Colton's Crossroad

A Sequel to Daniel's Obsession

Monica Collins

Publishing Coordinator – Sharon Kizziah-Holmes

Paperback-Press
an imprint of A & S Publishing
A & S Holmes, Inc.

ISBN -13: 978-1-956806-35-9

ACKNOWLEDGMENTS

From developing story lines, to editing, to proofreading, I have many people to thank for their assistance in the completion of this novel. I would like to thank Kirk Tyree, Shauna Evans, John and Teri Morris, Gayle Boles, Joan Fetter, Dusti Zang, Kati Thompson, Linda Hull and Allyn Collins for all of their helpful comments and suggestions.

CHAPTER ONE

In the past week, Robert Rucker's life had crumbled beneath him. As he stood, arms spread on either side of the kitchen sink, head lowered, he could think of nothing but the past horrendous week. His wife of almost twenty years died unexpectedly in her sleep. Robert's body wavered over the sink. The sadness in his heart was palpable. But his grief was not for his deceased wife, Margie, but for himself.

What was he to do? Be on the lookout for another woman to marry? The thought alone made him tired. He was no longer in shape. His haggard appearance had him looking ten years older than he actually was. His cozy routine of a perfectly scheduled life had been disrupted, and he was at a loss of what to do.

He thought briefly of his daughter, Marie. She would be ready to enter college next fall and had already submitted applications at several universities. He and Margie had saved some money for her higher education, but not nearly enough for four years at a major university. Marie would have to start at a nearby junior college. Either that, or she could go to beauty school. Robert didn't really care. Either way, Marie would soon leave their home, and he would have no one to help him.

As Robert stood and moped, Marie came into the house. She saw her father in the kitchen.

"I heard you leave. You weren't gone long," she said.

"I ran some errands, that's all. Where have you been?"

"Some people came by to pay their respects to mom. I took them to the cemetery."

"You couldn't just give them directions?" Robert's question was rhetorical as he went to the refrigerator and opened the door. He moved some items around, then glanced at Marie over the top of the door. "Where's the strawberries?"

As Marie lay her sweater over a chair, the question had no meaning. She thought her father was talking to himself.

"You ate all the strawberries. When did you eat them?"

Then she remembered--Daniel King was in the refrigerator and scared her half to death when she walked into the kitchen. "Last night. I had to have a midnight snack."

Robert closed the refrigerator door and glared at his daughter. "What?"

"I'm sorry I ate them all," she said.

Robert approached Marie, his tongue pressed

hard against his teeth. He stared her down. Why would you lie to me?"

Marie was speechless. Her father's face was contorted menacingly. Her father had never hit her, never so much as raised a hand at her, but his strange expression was frightening.

"You didn't eat them last night. I saw them in there this morning before I left the house." He stood over her. His fierce glare trapped her in a web of suspicion. "Well?"

A heavy silence invaded the room. Marie remained mute. Robert's mind jumped to another track.

Did you let the people who came by in the house and fed them?"

Marie had to go with it. "Yes. They weren't here long, maybe fifteen minutes."

"So you knew them?"

Marie shrugged.

"Were they from town?"

Marie shook her head.

"Speak up, girl. I'm talking to you. How many were there?"

"Just two, daddy."

"A couple?" Speak up, dammit."

"A young man and his father."

Robert had to think. "What the hell. You telling me you let two strange men in the house because they knew your mother died? How stupid can you get, Marie? They could have told you they were selling Bibles, then tied you up, molested you, and I don't know what else."

"I felt they were sincere."

"And you fed them a fruit dish. You think I was born yesterday? Who were they, Marie?"

"I didn't get names, daddy. He just said he was an old friend of mom's."

Robert sucked up a huge breath, "You're so disappointing, Marie." He paused and took another deep breath. "I've got enough on my mind right now so I don't want to hear any more about your mother being gone. You know, you don't have to open the door to strangers. Your mother's dead and buried." Even he didn't like the sound of what he'd said and he rubbed his face with two hands. "What I mean Marie--anyone who wants to know about your mother can go to the funeral home for information."

He walked right past his daughter headed for his bedroom.

CHAPTER TWO

W hen Daniel King made it back to Dallas, his adopted son Colton was already at the house. For Daniel, the two-and-a-half-day journey made him an older man, certainly wiser. He realized his life, to now, had been a gentle slope of life's ups and downs. Now his future was about to experience a rapid descent, and the toughest days of his life and most heart-breaking confessions were in front of him.

His daughters, Melissa and Morgan met him at the door with smiling faces. Colton and Daniel's wife, Brenda, remained seated at the kitchen table. Their faces were grim. Brenda rolled an empty coffee cup in her hands. Colton may have told Brenda about Margie, but even Colton didn't fully know all the trouble his father was in.

Daniel would have to confess everything to Brenda. She had always been so loyal, so steadfast, so supportive. Daniel spoke a quiet prayer to himself. He needed Brenda now, more than ever, and he was terrified the confessions that faced him would finally drive her away.

"Daddy's back," he said as he hugged the girls. He stepped to the kitchen doorway. "Anything for breakfast?"

"There's some coffee," Brenda said without moving from her chair.

Daniel poured himself a cup.

"I only came by to wait until you got back," Colton said. "I need to go ."

"Thanks for coming after me, son. It was a sad trip that accomplished nothing. I know that now, but I really appreciate you coming after me."

"So what happened that was so important you drove 200 miles to find out?" Brenda asked.

"I'll tell you later, dear. I'll tell you everything."

"He wanted to see his old girlfriend," Colton replied. He wasn't going to let his father cut any more corners. The days of being evasive and telling half-truths to his mother were over.

Daniel said nothing and bowed his head, and remained silent. Melissa and Morgan listened intently as did Brenda.

"We found out she had died unexpectedly."

Brenda immediately looked relieved.

"We met her daughter. She told us. . . I'd say, a closed chapter. What kind of secrets we keep," Colton waxed philosophical.

"It was hardly a secret," Brenda said as she got up from the table. "Do you want some breakfast?"

"Yes dear, I would, and yes it's a closed chapter."

Brenda gave Colton a look as Daniel's head was still down that said--'she wasn't through with this matter.' Her husband had thrown the memory of another woman into her family's tranquility. Her children now knew of his emotional infidelity, and the secret, now thrown in her lap was a slap in the face she was loath to endure. Daniel would get a piece of her mind real soon as she masked her hurt with a piercing stare.

"Okay then, I have to go," Colton said and he hugged the girls on his way out.

On his way to his apartment, Colton recounted all that happened the last few days. There was the confrontation with his birth father. He thought they might come to blows. He wanted Heath Diebold out of his life permanently. The man had spent fifteen years in prison for domestic violence that ended with his mother's death. Colton wanted nothing to do with the man.

When that matter was dealt with, at least temporarily, he no sooner woke up the following morning, and he was on a 200 mile trip to Spinler, Texas, to save his adopted father, Daniel, from himself. Once he got to town, he was thrown in the local jail for asking too many questions in the middle of the night.

Colton hoped the passing of his lost love would give his father closure. He prayed just as fervently, that the woman's unexpected death might give his mother some peace and relief, as well. His mother obviously knew about her husband's lingering memory. Maybe now his father's bouts of depression would end. Everyone in the family knew he went through days of uninterrupted sadness.

Now they all knew why. For Colton, the notion that his adoptive mother was the victim of torn affection was unsettling. He had always thought of Daniel in the best light both as a police officer and father, until now. The fact that he had been unfaithful to Brenda, if not physically, then certainly emotionally left a bad taste in his mouth. If anyone deserved to be loved unconditionally, it was his adoptive mother. Colton found it hard to reconcile the idea that his father was so duplicitous.

But then, Colton thought of a pretty school girl he met in Spinler. Her face was so expressive. She looked so young, but acted quite proper. A distinctive maturity about her had him especially curious. Her voice, her presence made his heart beat faster. He had never felt such a sensation before. It made no difference, nor would he pay it any mind, that the girl was the daughter of the woman who had broken his father's heart twenty years ago, and thereafter haunted his dreams. Colton could hardly wait until Saturday when he would travel back to Spinler, Texas, to see Marie again.

CHAPTER THREE

In the afternoon, after a shower and a nap, Daniel went to Brenda. "I'd like to take you to dinner tonight, hon, if you'd like to go out."

Brenda appeared sad, a bit dazed after all that had gone on.

"You deserve a night out, and I know it. I don't want you to feel bad when it's all my fault. Dinner and a hotel room. What do you say?"

Her blue eyes seemed to brighten. She even tried to smile. "I think that would be nice, Daniel."

"I had in mind the glass tower at the Hyatt Regency. I've been up to the top once. Spectacular view, of course. Then we'll get the honeymoon suite. Sauna, massage, breakfast in bed."

"Oh Daniel. You're so silly. What say we eat somewhere on Greenville Avenue, stay at a Holiday Inn, and cut the cost by more than half."

"Whatever you want, hon." And Daniel took her in his arms, and gave her a long, warm kiss.

They ate dinner at a Mexican restaurant on north

Greenville. A guitar and a violin played music among the diners. Daniel spoke of Brenda's wonderful traits, her role as the steadfast rudder for the family, all the while keeping his attention on her. He wanted her to feel cared about and safe. He wanted her to forgive him, but the plea never came. To truly forget Margie, he couldn't speak of her at all. He couldn't bring himself to speak of Margie anyway. He prayed Brenda could let it go, if not now, then in time.

Daniel thought it was a perfect meal. He hoped Brenda was comforted by his words. He had much more devastating news to tell Brenda when they got to their room than any news about the passing of a college lover.

Brenda's smile was in full display when they arrived at the Hampton Inn, her eyes bright and happy. Daniel ordered room service for a bottle of Merlot. They helped each other undress. They both enjoyed the choreography. When they slipped into bed, Daniel's hand under her lower back, they began to move in rhythm. Daniel knew every part of her body. And he knew what she especially liked, nibbles on the neck. Daniel moved slowly and lovingly. He enjoyed the intimacy, but problematic thoughts held center court in his mind. He would have to tell Brenda tonight, and turn himself in tomorrow. If he didn't, the hour was soon at hand when the authorities would be knocking at his door.

As they lay in each other's arms, satisfied and spent, Daniel kissed Brenda on the cheek and said to her, "Dear, there's something I must tell you." Brenda rolled toward him, and put her head on his chest.

Daniel fell asleep. When he awoke, he saw he'd napped for just over an hour. Brenda was dressed in her nightgown, and was combing her hair in front of the bathroom mirror.

Daniel slipped out of bed and put on his shorts and a T-shirt.

Brenda walked into the bedroom. "So what were you going to tell me, Mr. King?" Her expression was one of contentment, but her eyes held a hint of apprehension.

Daniel pulled on his pants and sat at a table. "Come sit with me, hon." He reached both hands across the table. She reached with one hand, and hesitantly placed it in the curl of his fingers.

"Sweetheart, I met Colton and Morgan on a police call, as you know, more than a year before I met you. When I saw those poor children, I was emotionally torn, honey." He swallowed involuntarily and began again. "I began targeting men who had beaten their female partners."

Brenda's expression changed from contentment to concern, but he could tell she didn't yet grasp the gravity of his confession.

"From police records I learned who had been convicted of domestic violence. From my own experience, I ran into even more men who treated their families like punching bags, especially their wives."

Brenda pulled her hand away, and glared at him.

"In my off hours, I sought out men and beat them with their own belts or otherwise terrorized them for their physical violence against their own family members."

Brenda was now one step ahead of him. "And you're telling me this now because . . . ?"

"Someone identified me. The detective in charge has my scent. I'm pretty sure the department has others who will back that up." He shook his head, dejected and resigned. "Assault and battery is a felony. There's no justification for what I did outside the law."

Brenda rubbed her head, totally at a loss for words. "You did what?" It took her a moment to register the news, but when she faced him again the sweet, loving Brenda was gone. "You're going to lose your job? Good grief, Daniel. How are we going to pay our bills?"

She paced the bedroom. "But it's more than that, isn't it? You're going to be prosecuted?"

Daniel nodded, his body drenched in shame and remorse.

"You are a cop. Dammit, how could you be so stupid? What about me and the girls? Huh? Where does that leave us?" Brenda sat on the edge of the bed and rubbed the bridge of her nose. "For fifteen years I've been your nursemaid, nanny, give you a pill, get you a drink. I'm sick of it. Grow up will you. I don't care why you went after those 'whoever they are,' use your brain." Brenda walked around the room again.

"I should have known this night out wasn't because you care about me, but to butter me up for your incessant bad news. Well, I've had it up to here. My husband, a nice upstanding cop, is going to jail. I'll tell you one thing right now. You stay

12

right here for the night. I'm going back to the house."

Within ten minutes, Brenda was out the hotel room door. Daniel remained seated at the table with the knowledge that his troubles had just begun.

CHAPTER FOUR

A week after Margie Rucker's funeral, her husband, Robert, began going through her things. She had a significant wardrobe. Robert wasn't inclined to give her dresses away or waste time trying to sell them. He would keep all of her clothes for now. She had a fantasy sort of book on her nightstand. The cover was full of color, a fairy waving a wand that swept the surface with a trail of stars. Robert threw the book in the trash.

Robert went through her dresser. The jewelry on top he dumped into a box, and put it on a shelf in his closet. The bras, panties, slips, and pantyhose he threw away. Nobody wants to wear another person's underclothes. There was a blanket in the bottom drawer and he left it there.

As he scanned the bedroom, he saw something sticking out from under her mattress. It was a notebook. He opened it without giving any thought as to what it contained. Notations--a ledger? A diary? No, these were letters. To her mother possibly? Letters written but not sent. He flipped through the pages, then picked one at random, and began to read. It was Margie's handwriting, of that he was sure. He finished reading the first one.

The letter said nothing, trivial musings of Margie's mind. 'Hope you're doing well,' wish I knew you were okay.' 'I've got my beautiful daughter to keep me going.'

Robert read another letter. It was all crap. What did she have, some nebulous pen pal in the sky? Damn that woman. All along, she was thinking about another man. Reflexively, he grabbed a hand mirror from the bureau, and threw it across the room where it shattered against the far wall. He tossed her mattress off the box springs and there was something else hidden under the bed. Robert snatched the Manila envelope, and shook out the contents. Dozens of pictures of Margie back in her college days.

A fury overtook him. The top of his head began to throb, and he thought he better lie down. For a moment he couldn't catch his breath. The anger that boiled inside him was more than his system could stand.

The disloyal bitch. After all he had done for her-- bought her a house, gave her a daughter, kept her financially secure. Robert closed his eyes and took deep breaths, yet his frame of mind didn't allow him to consider that with Margie's untimely passing, that chapter in his life should be over.

No! He would make the man pay who had held her heart. He got up from his resting position, and went into the den. He spread the notebook open on a table where sunlight came through the window. There, he could see better, and he began to read every other letter. They all amounted to the same thing. Love letters to someone who would never know Margie wrote them. But what filled Robert's heart with rage was the fact that Margie had written them at all.

Robert knew what the capital M meant at the end of each letter. But what was the capital D at the beginning of each one? Robert didn't have to deceive himself, and pretend he didn't know. He knew. The D stood for Daniel. He'd forgotten the man's last name, but he knew enough. The thought crossed his mind that the two of them may have been communicating for years. Margie didn't mail these letters, but had she gotten similar ones from this guy? If so, she had probably hidden them deep in her closet. Robert grabbed a beautiful porcelain figurine of a horse with its front hooves in the air from the shelf and smashed it on the floor. Margie had picked it up at a fair when she was a little girl. It had been her favorite knickknack.

He rushed to the bedroom, grabbed a stool, and pulled down everything on the shelves above Margie's hang-up clothes--shoe boxes, a box of Christmas ornaments, another box of Marie's kindergarten drawings and the like, several photo albums (most of the pictures were of Marie) and a box of copies of previous year's tax returns. Robert dumped the box of Marie's schoolwork on the floor. After fifteen minutes of searching through a child's grade school homework, he gave up. None of the boxes contained any letters. But for Robert, the lack of correspondence didn't prove innocence. He now had it in his mind that his wife was having an affair.

Margie and Daniel could have been talking on the phone for years, and he would never have known. He now wondered if the man lived in Spinler. They could have been meeting together for short flings, and he would never have suspected. The thought made the back of his eyes hurt. It was as if the blood flow in his body was being pumped so powerfully it was tearing holes in his brain. He picked up all the papers, threw them back in the box, and carried it out to the garbage can.

Back in the house, he sat and rubbed his face with both hands. Just over a week ago--he recalled with vivid revulsion the events of that morning. Sunlight peeked through the blinds. He got up to use the restroom. It was Sunday morning. He had every intention of crawling back into bed and sleeping until noon. But when he returned to the bedroom, the way Margie lay in her bed was disconcerting. She was on her stomach. More than half her face was buried in the pillow. Her right arm hung over the bed and touched the floor. Robert went to her side and pulled back the covers. He touched her shoulder, intending to turn her over. Her skin was cold to the touch. He jumped back, and felt the dump of bile fill his guts as his brain registered the sight before him. He could tell she wasn't breathing. He took hold of her her dangling arm in an attempt to turn her over. He knew she was dead.

The arm was stiff, and her body moved in one piece as he pushed her onto her back.

Dry heaves climbed up his throat, and his body wretched beside the bed. He took a step back and couldn't believe the sight in front of him. Margie's face was a waxy blue. She had vomited all over her pillow. Some of her tongue hung out of the corner of her mouth.

It wasn't the sight that was terrifying, but the realization. There was a corpse in his bedroom. What if they'd still been sleeping together. The dead person was no longer his Margie, nothing but deadmeat, and he gagged again. Robert stumbled to his nightstand, and dialed 911.

To lose his wife, an otherwise healthy woman, at the age of thirty-nine devastated him. But an even more crushing blow was the knowledge that his wife had saved her heart for another man. Robert found himself in the pit of despair. He would find out what transpired between the two of them. He would track the man down. The man had violated the sanctity of a loving marriage. Robert would find him and make him pay.

CHAPTER FIVE

W hen Colton left Dallas on a 200-mile trip to Spinler to track down Daniel, he had no idea why his father had headed there or what he would find once he arrived. His father, Daniel King, had been on a desperate quest to see a long, lost love one more time. As fate would have it, the woman had died less than ten days earlier.

As his father had mourned the woman's passing at the cemetery, Colton talked with her daughter, Marie Rucker. Colton was immediately smitten by her beauty and her wit. They made a date for the following weekend. Colton would again make the 200-mile trip. this time to see a girl who had captured his eye and curiosity. What more was there to that darling creature?

Colton arrived at her front door in the afternoon at the appointed time. The door was answered by her father.

"Good afternoon, sir. Is Marie home?"

Robert's expression was one of pure boredom. He had never seen the young man before. He looked too old to be in high school. Robert was about to ask a question when Marie rushed to the door.

"Thanks, daddy. This is Colton. We're going to drive out to the lake. I won't be gone too long."

Once in his pick-up, Colton said, "My, you look happy."

"I am happy. Happy to get out of this town for a while. Happy to see you." Marie reached over and touched his hand.

"You have a pretty smile," he said.

"Thank you. I saved it all for you."

Her voice brought music to his ears, and a thrilling feeling to his chest he'd never felt before. When they reached the highway, Colton said, "You can sit closer if you like." And Marie did. A mile later down the road, Colton put his arm behind her head, and rested his hand on her shoulder..

"Yes, that is more comfortable," she said, and she lay her head against him.

"How's your father doing?" she asked.

Colton sighed, "Do you really want to know?"

Marie looked up at him. "Well, yes. He seemed to be a nice man."

"He's taken your mother's death really hard. He says otherwise, but I can tell different. And I know why. In the twenty-some years since they were in college my dad has made a shrine to your mother in his mind. It's kind of pathological. It's also sad."

My sister told me my parents had a fight. I've never known them to yell at each other. But--my dad has other issues. I'm afraid he may lose his job as a police officer. So, it hasn't been good."

"How about you?" she asked.

20

Colton glanced down at her. "I'm doing fine. I didn't drive all the way down here because I didn't have anything better to do. I came to see you. Right now, I'm doing just fine."

"Me too," she said, and she snuggled closer to him.

"We should be in Austin in an hour."

Until now, Colton had lived his life by the strict demarcations of the calendar and the clock. His time had been taken up with schooling, then work. Free time was spent helping out his sister, Morgan, which meant helping his adoptive parents, the Kings, and their daughter, Melissa.

He wasn't a virgin, having been seduced by an older woman, a housewife whose air conditioner he'd repaired. Colton was handsome and polite, a prize for women young or older. Every inch of six foot tall, Colton had the body of a man, but his face hadn't been streaked with age or burnt by the sun. If a woman could turn his head, she would lead him to a bed.

Colton was not assertive in that he had to have his own way about everything. If another person's decision about something was practical and safe, Colton would quietly go along with it. On the other hand, if someone wanted to drive across a flooded road, he would quickly object. Neither was he assertive when it came to asking a girl out to a movie or a school dance. He was approachable, and determined girls would do so. Then they would direct Colton's thoughts to the matter at hand, and get him to ask them out. But for Colton, all was just a matter of being respectful and polite.

But in the last week, Colton's perspective changed. A petite high school girl from Spinler, Texas, focused his thoughts. His perception of the world around him changed. Clarity came to his thinking, and he saw the future in his mind's eye. The very thought of Marie made him happy. Now, with his arm over her shoulders, and her head resting against his chest, Colton wanted to know everything about her. He knew he could gaze at her across a table for an hour and not say a word. He could swim in the brilliance of her bright blue eyes, and bask in the warmth of her presence. At the moment, he never wanted to let her go.

Marie rested her head against Colton's shoulder. She was in the arms of a man she barely knew who was taking her out of town. She had never been out of Spinler except with her parents, and on a school field trip. But her heart felt both peaceful and thrilled. The young man, five years her senior, was attentive and poised. She sensed his maturity. For now, Marie anxiously awaited a fun-filled evening joining the revelers on the Saturday night streets of Austin, Texas. But unconsciously, another little voice whispered at the back of her mind, she may have found a man worth holding tight.

They got back to Spinler at two in the morning. Colton parked at the entrance to the driveway, went around, opened the truck door for her, then pulled her to himself in a brief but passionate hug.

"Can I see you again?" he asked.

"How about next Saturday?" she said, her eyes sparkling in the moonlight.

"I guess we could go bowling."

She smiled. "Oh, Saturday night would be awfully hard to get a lane, but we could always go out and eat."

"I'll be here at six on the dot." Colton pulled her close again. "Goodnight. I had a great time, Marie" He released her, leaned back against his truck, and waited for her to get into the house.

He didn't even try to kiss me, she thought. Marie could think of nothing she wanted more. To deny her the touch of his lips was, at that moment, standing in the cool night air, a first date propriety she could not bear.

"It was a wonderful evening, Colton," and she stood on tiptoes, and kissed his cheek.

He leaned over, put his arms about her back, lifted her slightly, and placed a warm, tender kiss upon her lips. Then he took her hand and walked her to the door. "There'll be another one of those next week," he said.

Marie took a deep breath and fumbled with her house key. "Good night, Colton. I had a wonderful evening." Once inside, Marie made her way by memory through the darkened rooms. She was about at her bedroom door when it seemed every light in the house came on at once, and Marie saw her father sitting in his recliner in the den.

"Kinda late, Marie, wouldn't you say?"

She was instantly struck mute because she hadn't anticipated a confrontation with her father.

"I don't know how late your mother let you stay out, but I don't think it was past midnight. Where have you been?"

Marie approached her father. "I'm fine, daddy. Nothing happened. It's late because of the drive. We went to Austin."

"What the hell for?"

"Saturday night. There's a lot going on downtown on Saturday nights."

"What? Like drinking and carousing, and using dope?"

"No, no. We didn't do any of that. Colton wouldn't even drink a beer since I could only order soft drinks."

"Who exactly is that boy anyway? How'd you meet him?"

A little birdie told Marie she needed to pull her punches with these questions. Colton was indirectly connected to her deceased mother. She could never mention the existence of Colton's father.

"At the gas station. He asked me if I knew someone, I don't remember who. I realize now he was just making conversation, but we got to talking and he asked me out."

"You talked to a total stranger at a gas station long enough to feel comfortable to go out with him. That doesn't sound real smart, Marie. What's his last name?"

"I didn't ask. I'm tired. Can I go to bed?"

"Yes, but listen up. As long as you're in high school, you will be in this house no later than ten p.m. every day. Am I clear?"

"Yes, yes daddy. I won't be out late again."

CHAPTER SIX

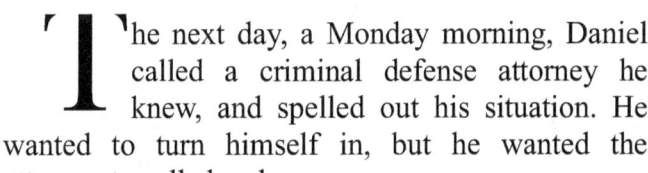

The next day, a Monday morning, Daniel called a criminal defense attorney he knew, and spelled out his situation. He wanted to turn himself in, but he wanted the attorney to call ahead.

"Talk to detective Mike Sanders. He knows the details. He's probably in front of a judge right now getting a warrant signed."

"I know him," the attorney said. "Why don't you come to my office? I'll make some phone calls and we'll go to the station together."

Ultimately, Daniel was charged with twenty-three counts of assault and battery. He eventually bonded out of jail. The trial would begin in eight weeks.

The story made The Dallas Morning News--

Domestic Vigilante Identified
Ex-Cop Faces Charges

Daniel's criminal trial lasted a week. The DA put ten men on the stand who recited similar versions of the 'I got my ass whipped because had to take on someone my own size,' grousing. 'He ambushed me,' 'He invaded my home.' Daniel didn't recognize half of them.

Brenda didn't attend any of the sessions. Morgan and Melissa attended them all.

The newspaper's coverage brought more than a dozen calls of women willing to testify for the defense. Over a dozen women knew about the case, knew about Daniel's attack on their male partners, and wanted to tell their stories. The court allowed three witnesses to testify for the defense.

"I knew someone had beat the shit out of Darrel, pardon my language, judge. He had welts all over his back, I had to put ointment on it for days, and he'd wear two shirts to bed so it wouldn't get it all over everything, and he slept on his stomach. He had been slapping me around for more than ten years over any little thing, whether he'd been drinking or not. He could be in a bad mood, and hit me so hard it would knock me to the floor. Most of the time, he'd hit me in the back so I wouldn't see it coming. I don't know what, if any, words were exchanged when he got beat, but he hasn't laid a hand on me in the two years since it happened."

The jury came back with a guilty verdict. Daniel and his attorney stood before the judge.

"Mr. King-- I must tell you I have never seen a case anywhere close to this in my twenty years on the bench." The judge made direct eye contact with

Daniel. "You were trained to protect and serve. There are no provisions that allow you or anyone else to apply their own version of justice.

"Except for death penalty cases, and even there, the sentence is carried out humanely, does the law allow anything other than incarceration as punishment in this country. Many people have their eyes opened when they lose their freedom. But loss of personal freedom is, as it should be, society's only recourse, Mr. King. We don't beat, whip, or flog people for their crimes."

The judge paused to let his words sink in.

"I am ready to pronounce sentence. Because of your otherwise exemplary record and the fact that no one was robbed or killed, I hereby sentence you to the minimum sentence mandated by Texas statute. Mr. Daniel King, you are hereby sentenced to three to five years in the Texas Department of Corrections. This court is in recess."

CHAPTER SEVEN

---◆---

Thanksgiving was on the calendar between the time Daniel turned himself in to authorities, and his trial date. For a time, Brenda let Daniel languish in jail. She would bail him out before the trial, but he had only himself to blame for his predicament. It made her furious that she would have part with close to two grand to the bail bondsman just to let him walk free for a few weeks. Based on what he had told her, Brenda seriously doubted he would be found not guilty.

Brenda wanted Thanksgiving to be a quiet affair with her and her children. If Daniel were free, it would be an incessant rehashing of his problems, and she didn't want to hear it. Besides, Colton had said he would like to bring a girl to their Thanksgiving dinner. The idea pleased Brenda. She was more than curious to know who Colton was seeing.

Colton made their second date. He drove the

four-hundred-mile round trip to have chicken fried steaks with Marie at The Spinler Diner.They could have been eating at the Four Seasons Club Room, and the evening would not have been more enjoyable. Marie began saying Colton's name in a drawn-out, two-syllable expression of endearment. They were both hypnotized by the other, but equally practical. Marie couldn't leave home; not yet. Colton couldn't leave his place of work; not yet. But seeing each other on any kind of regular basis living two hundred miles apart was unsustainable.

"Would you like to come to Dallas with me for Thanksgiving?" he asked.

"Oh yes, that would be nice."

Marie didn't know if she was in love. She was old enough to revel in Colton's attention, but was still naive about the world around her. She knew best to keep her passions in check. She would not freely give her body to any man. During their bouts of making out, Colton respected boundaries, and Marie sensed it. She trusted Colton.

She had planned to go to college. Her mother's death left those plans spinning in uncertainty.

The idea of one day living in Dallas excited her, but she knew such plans, at this time, were nothing more than wishful thinking.

What did Colton think about their possible future together? She knew he was too pragmatic to not have given it some thought. He treated her like a priceless porcelain vase. That alone told her he was not out to take advantage of her. During their time together, their gazes seldom left the other's face.

Colton's speech was slow and measured. He wasn't much on chit-chat. But Marie could read his face like a newspaper headline. He was good looking, intelligent, and she had captured his full attention.

Colton drove to Spinler the night before, stayed in a motel, then picked up Marie on Thanksgiving for the trip to Dallas.

"I can't wait to meet your family," she said,

"You'll like my sisters. Morgan is a little older than you. Melissa is fourteen, I think. Morgan is my real sister. We were adopted by the Kings. You'll really like my mom, too."

"Adopted? You didn't tell me about that."

Colton looked her way, and reached for her hand. "It's not that big a deal, but it's not a conversation for today."

"That's okay," she said. "I'm not in a hurry to learn all about you." Marie cocked her head in her mischievous way, and a sparkle in her eyes accompanied a smile..

"There's something though I better tell you before we get to the house," Colton said. "My mom knows a few things about your mother so don't mention that you're from Spinler. Let's say you're from Round Rock. The whole episode of my father's obsession with a college sweetheart had been hard on my mom. She learned bits and pieces of it over the years. How could she not? I hope you understand?"

"Yes, I understand. My dad wanted me to tell him all about you after we went to Austin. I felt it was better not to, and I didn't."

Colton smiled at her, and brushed back her rich

black hair from her forehead. "My mom may know your last name, too. Can you come up with another last name?"

"Sure," Marie said. "I'll use my mother's maiden name, Winters."

"Crap," Colton blurted out and smacked the steering wheel. "The girls are going to want to know how we met, and everything else about you. I hate to be telling a bunch of lies."

Marie touched his arm. "We'll just stick with what we've already decided, nothing more."

"You don't know my sisters."

"Don't worry, Sweetheart. You are my sweetheart, you know. We're going to have a lovely afternoon."

They walked into the house to a warm greeting from the three women. Brenda's happy expression slowly receded as she took a second look at Marie. She had seen that face before, and recently. While Daniel was in jail, Brenda had gone through all of his things whether they were supposedly private or not. There would be no more lingering vestiges of Margie Rucker in her home. In one ragged manila envelope, Brenda found over a hundred pictures of a young woman. She assumed they were pictures of her husband's lost love. She had looked at half the pictures and thrown them all away. But now, in her living room was another young woman, the spitting image of the woman in the photos. And how long had it been since Colton said he'd met a new girlfriend--less than a month ago--just about the same time he had followed his father down to

Spinler.

While the table was being set, Colton and Marie watched the Thanksgiving Day parade on TV while the girls helped Brenda. When they all took their seats, Colton said a prayer. He wasn't used to saying prayers aloud in a group, but today he was truly thankful. He spoke from the heart. All the women said an approving amen when he finished.

The table was set with a huge turkey and all the fixings. Everyone passed bowls and filled their plates.

"So where do you go to school?" Melissa asked. She was eager for information about her big brother's new girlfriend. Though not blood related, Melissa loved Colton as no other little sister could-- a shining star of manhood. She hoped her future held a man like Colton. She had blonde hair and a slightly broad nose like her mother, Brenda. Her smile was full of laughter, and her blue eyes abrim with fun.

"I'm still in high school," Marie said. "I'm a senior." Melissa and Morgan exchanged glances.

Morgan ate a bite of green bean casserole, and eyed the couple across the table. Now twenty-one and a junior in college, Morgan's thick brown hair matched the color of her eyes, and ran down her back. Her eyes seemed back lit by stars. With such a friendly facial expression Morgan made everyone around feel at ease. But when she was relaxed in a contemplative air of silent repose, Morgan's visage was as stunning as any goddess of ancient Greece.

"You have to watch Colton like a hawk," Morgan said. "One minute he's docile as a puppy, and the next minute as wild as a bucking bronc." Her infectious smile gave away her intent.

Marie caught the expression. "Oh, he's no problem. If he gets out of line, I give him a kiss. That gets his attention."

Melissa giggled. Brenda ate slowly and listened intently. Colton playfully rolled his eyes.

"I plan to go to college next fall."

"Where at?" Morgan asked.

"Haven't decided yet. I've made an application to a few schools, but I have all of next spring to work that out."

"What do your parents do?" Brenda chimed in.

"Mother, all the questions. Can't we just eat?"

On the surface, Colton's statement was reasonable, but his tone said something else. His sisters looked at each other again. Colton reached out and touched his mother's arm. "I'm sorry if I sounded harsh, mom. There will be plenty of time to get to know Marie."

Brenda went back to cutting the turkey on her plate. Colton was hiding something--she knew it. But the reason was plainly evident. The adorable girl at her dinner table had a recognizable face. Brenda would no longer accept games of self-delusion that had haunted her marriage for years. She would not allow Colton to lie to her because she already knew--her son was dating the daughter of the woman whose memory had destroyed her husband.

CHAPTER EIGHT

eath Diebold walked the streets of Northeast Dallas. He did enough to keep from being fired from his warehouse job. He was forty-five pushing sixty. For years he'd abused his body using his bare fingers as tools, opening beer bottles with his teeth, and taking showers maybe once a month when he began to stink so bad even he couldn't stand to be around himself. When he wasn't working, Heath spent his time pilfering unlocked cars like they were dumpsters free to rummage.

Heath was Colton and Morgan's birth father. His domestic violence cost their mother her life, and Heath spent fifteen years in the penitentiary for his crime.

In the weeks that had passed since Daniel and Colton had confronted him not to contact either Colton or Morgan, Heath seethed with indignation. Colton and Morgan were his kids regardless of the fact they'd been adopted. Their last name was now

King--not an uncommon name, but there shouldn't be so many that Heath couldn't track them down.

Heath was unaware that Daniel was currently in jail facing multiple assault charges. His immediate goal was to see his daughter, Morgan. She would be about twenty-one, and he hadn't seen her in a decade and a half. The girl had written him a few letters while in prison, but never came to visit. No one was going to tell him he couldn't see his own daughter.

Heath Diebold had the common sense of a fly that repeatedly crashes into a glass pane in order to escape, only to finally die and fall on the window sill. And yet, there was a shrewdness about him. He had streetwise intuition, and a risk-averse attitude. Fifteen years in the slammer hadn't quelled his appetite for ill-conceived behavior.

Heath knew little about the internet, but a couple named Cook who lived near the old motel property where he stayed had a computer. Heath had seen it, a little fold up they carried around. They ran a porn shop several blocks from the motel with peep shows and a limited selection of DVDs. Their main draw was the scantily dressed strippers who danced inside plastic cylindrical tubes each with its own color scheme-- sky blue, bright yellow, pink, light green, and purple. For $25 a voyeur could ogle the physical attributes of a pretty female for as long as it took four mind-numbing old ballads to play.

Heath bought them each a pack of smokes, and they agreed to do an internet search for all the King's in the Dallas area. The search came back with 237 names. Mike Cook printed him off a list.

Heath left with the list, unsure of his next move.

There were addresses attached to each name, but many were post office boxes. Even if they had all been street address, there were far too many to investigate individually. What was that guy's name-- the man who had come with Colton to intimidate him against further contact with his birth children? Heath couldn't remember the man's first name, if he had ever heard it. The name was likely on the list. If only he could cut down the number. He went back to his housing unit, and began scanning the list.

After Thanksgiving dinner, Colton took a nap. The three young women chatted about everything and nothing. Marie told them all they wanted to know about her, and Colton without divulging anything important. When Colton got up, he took the girls to a movie, the new release of True Grit starring Jeff Bridges.

When Colton and Marie prepared to leave there were hugs all around. The girls were already best friends with Marie. She had landed their brother. Besides, Morgan was too friendly to wish anything but the best for them. Melissa was enthralled by the very idea of dating. She thought Marie was the luckiest girl in the world.

Brenda hugged Colton as the last person to see him out the door. "Drive careful to Spinler," she whispered in his ear.

Colton turned and moved quickly down the steps, but the message had hit home. His mother knew. It irked him that she would blatantly jam a splinter into the enjoyable afternoon. He and Marie had been coy for the sole purpose of sparing her unpleasant memories. But it made no difference. She could know all about Marie's family, and throw it in his face whenever she wanted to pick a scab. But he wasn't his father, and Marie was not her mother. He was a grown man now. He would see Marie Rucker for as long as he wanted, whenever he wanted.

As they headed south on I-45, Colton spoke up. "My father is currently sitting in prison. He did some bad things related to his unhealthy longings for your mother."

"Oh, Colton. I'm sorry to hear that. I wondered why he wasn't at dinner. I knew you'd tell me sooner or later."

"I think we probably shouldn't see each other for a while."

"No."

"I'm going to need to help my mother now that he's gone."

"No, Colton. Christmas break is just weeks away. I can come to Dallas and stay at your apartment."

Colton glanced at Marie and shook his head. "You're not staying at my apartment during Christmas vacation.." He reached for her, and she turned toward the door.

"Marie--I have to be at work in the morning. I have to keep that job right now. I've got too many things to do. I can't be running down to Spinler every weekend.

Marie glared at him from the far side of the seat. "What's got into you?"

"Just for a while, babe. I need some time."

"Good grief, Colton. Is this how you let someone down? Throw them, a hand grenade after a lovely afternoon? Do I suddenly smell bad? Do I have a pimple on my lip?" She turned and began crying. She didn't sob or sniffle. Marie began bawling.

"Come over here, sweetie. I'm not leaving you. Please don't do that. I didn't mean it to come out that way."

For the next hundred miles, Marie kept to her side of the seat. Colton smiled to himself. She was being melodramatic like a young girl, but he knew her tears were real. She was also afraid--afraid of losing him. In that moment, Colton realized he loved her--the petite young woman with an angel's face from Spinler, Texas. Finally, she was exhausted, and put her head on his lap, and went to sleep. Colton put his hand on her shoulder, and thought about the wonderful day it had been, and he and Marie had gotten through their first fight.

CHAPTER NINE

In the weeks since his wife's death, Robert Rucker stepped back into his usual routine. Condolences from coworkers were less a comfort to his traumatized psyche, and more a festering replay of horrific memories. He wished they would all keep their shallow platitudes to themselves. Margie was gone and that was that. The time he had with Margie meant nothing to him now. He was barely forty-two years old. He wasn't going to spend the rest of his life wearing sackcloth and ashes over a dead woman.

Margie had betrayed him. She had been communicating with another man. The thought burned a hole in the center of his brain. Margie may have been in contact with this man during their entire marriage. Had they met for late afternoon rendezvous? The man, Daniel somebody, was probably too stupid or clumsy to get a woman of his own. At the moment, Robert cared nothing about his daughter, himself, or his deceased wife. Revenge filled his heart. He began to backtrack through his memory. Maybe there was some way to identify this Daniel, and find out exactly where he lived. Robert heard someone pull into the driveway, and he went to the spare bedroom window where he could see.

When Colton and Marie reached Spinler, Marie was still asleep. Colton went around, opened her door, and gently awakened her. "Time to get into real bed, angel." He helped her out of the truck. "I think I'll always call you angel from now on."

Marie smiled sleepily and hugged him. "Will you promise to always mention angel every night before you go to bed?"

"I promise."

"Please don't stay away too long."

"No longer than I have to." He picked her up from the ground, and kissed her as warm and as tenderly as he could. Their faces lingered at each other's lips as Marie held the sides of his head with both hands. They didn't want to let each other go. But finally, Colton placed her back on the ground, and walked her to the door.

"Sleep well, my angel."

Marie turned and went into the house.

From the window, Robert saw it all. Nothing Colton and Marie did in the driveway was inappropriate, but their passion raised many questions. He had seen the young man once, maybe twice before, but he knew nothing about him. The budding romance had flourished overnight. Robert needed to get answers. It was his responsibility as a father to do so.

He was back in his recliner when Marie walked in.

"Happy Thanksgiving," she said without prompt. "Did you get something to eat or would you like me to fix something? I'm sorry I didn't bring anything back."

"Yes, I got something to eat--Marie, who is that young man?"

"Haven't you met him?"

"At the door for two seconds before you pulled him away."

"I'll bring him in to speak with you next time he comes by."

"That's good, Marie. I'm just a . . . where did you go today? You left around 7:30. It's almost eight now. Austin again?"

"No, daddy. We went to Dallas."

"Dallas! Your boyfriend is becoming quite mysterious. Is that where he works?"

"Yes."

"You said you met him at the gas station, but I wondered--just days after your mother passed, you said two men came to the door."

"Yes daddy. We've been over this."

"Come over here," he told her. Robert set his focus on his daughter's face, every blink of her eyelids, any twitch of her nose or pursing of her lips. "A thought occurred to me earlier today. Those two guys you took to the cemetery weren't in town because they missed the funeral. They didn't even know your mother had died, did they?"

The question caught her like a punch to the

throat. Her facial features held tight, but she could feel the heat of her blushing—not from embarrassment or humiliation, but from the sheer panic of being in the cross hairs of his inquisition. He was putting two and two together too quickly. If her father ever knew for sure that the young man she was dating was the son of the man who had held his wife's affection all these years, he'd probably throw her out of the house.

"Humm," Robert said with an inflection of satisfaction. "So why were they here, Marie?"

"I didn't ask about that at the time, daddy. Maybe they were just passing through town, and they wanted to stop and say hi."

"Good grief, Marie. You're such a terrible liar. I'm positive now--they told you why they initially came to town." Robert rose from his recliner and paced the room. "You said, it was 'a young man and his father.' Is this how you met your new boyfriend?"

Marie inhaled a deep breath. Her father's interrogation made her mad. "Yes."

"It makes sense, being from Dallas. But why would two men take a long distance trip to little old Spinler?" Robert let his words settle in the room like a descending cloud. "What's his name?" Robert demanded.

"His name is Colton. I don't even know the other man."

"You said it was his father."

"I don't know, daddy."

"What's their last name?"

"I don't know. I don't know." Tears filled her

eyes, and she physically shrank against his accusations.

"Well, you'll never be able to keep up a relationship with a grown man who lives in Dallas. You can forget all that, I assure you. Concentrate on your studies, and high school graduation, Marie. That's the best road, don't you think?"

Marie looked at her father, utterly heartbroken at the moment and beyond upset. She darted to her bedroom without another word.

CHAPTER TEN

B renda was crushed when Daniel was found guilty. Although she hadn't attended any court sessions, she wanted a full recount each day from the girls about what had transpired. They told her about the three women who the court let testify for the defense. The women were sincere and thankful. The unlawful thrashings manifested a welcome change in their husbands. But their stories meant nothing to the law.

The judge mentioned Daniel's fine record as a police officer in his closing statement, but that too, had no bearing on the case.

Brenda had been mad at Daniel, truly upset with all his half-truths. He had never let her fully into his heart, and she resented it. When the sentence was passed, however, she became a shadow of her former self. The thought of being alone after all these years left her catatonic with indecision. She had been a stay-at-home mom ever since Melissa was born and Colton and Morgan were adopted.

She had depended and counted on a breadwinner, a provider and protector--a husband. How would she get by the next three to five years? If this was her midlife crisis, it was devastating. She despised Daniel, and longed for him at the same time. She thought of divorce or selling the house and moving. But at age forty-eight she knew, she was tethered to an unstable man who had left her alone to be buffeted about by the winds of life.

She was never especially attractive. She had no special skills. Their savings would have to be seriously depleted just to get by. She knew her children would help all they could, but it wouldn't be the same without a man around the house.

She lay in bed for three days, despondent and discouraged. The girls understood the situation and did what they could to cheer her up. Maybe the upcoming Christmas holidays would renew her spirit, and get her mind on more pleasant things.

CHAPTER ELEVEN

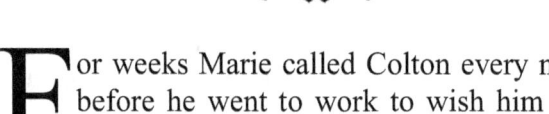

For weeks Marie called Colton every morning before he went to work to wish him a great day. Evening phone conversations could be lengthy. Colton let her talk. Marie was never short of interesting tidbits. You would have thought from her excited elaborations that the little town of Spinler, Texas, was as festive as Times Square.

She asked about him in a sincere, caring way. She missed him, that was evident in her voice, but she didn't sound needy. He appreciated that. He fully intended to care for, and be attentive to, the woman who became his wife. Yet, he didn't want a female that needed continual hand holding to feel validated. Marie was bright, beautiful, and a fast learner. Colton leaned back in quiet contentment as he listened to her talk.

Colton asked for two days off work in the middle of the week. The request was granted and he left early the following morning, luggage packed for several days. Upon arriving, he spent several hours visiting the two heating and air conditioning businesses in Spinler. Either one would hire him whenever he became available. Then he went to the high school, and walked into the office.

"Good afternoon," he said. "I wanted to locate Marie Rucker."

"And you are?" the woman behind the counter asked.

"A friend from Dallas. My name's Colton." His bright blue eyes, and relaxed posture may have encouraged the woman to be helpful for she leaned closer to him and said.

"Classes aren't out until three. I can't tell you what room she's in, but--just a moment let me see." She flipped through a file cabinet. "Based on where her last class and her locker is, I'd say she'll come out the front door to leave the building. You're welcome to wait outside."

"Thank you so much. You're as sweet as Marie."

The middle-aged woman took it all in stride with a gleam in her eyes. "You're welcome."

Colton had almost two hours to kill, but he needn't leave and had no desire to do so. For a while he sat on the bike rack, then under an elm tree, and played with the sticks and leaves that had fallen.

When the doors burst open, and a throng of adolescent humanity surged outside, Colton watched intently for the girl that had won his heart.

Marie was in the middle of the pack, walking leisurely, talking to a friend. When she got within earshot, Colton called out, "Has anyone seen Marie Rucker?"

She turned and looked, dropped her books, and rushed into his arms. She clung to him and kissed his face and neck, then planted her lips on his. "Oh darling, what a wonderful surprise."

"Dallas is so big and lonely without you," he said as he gazed into her eyes. "Let's go get something to eat." When he let her down, she continued to hug his chest. "Let's get your books."

As they walked to his truck, Marie, excited and thrilled, knew she had to check her enthusiasm. Hug and kiss him, but don't fawn all over him. Don't be overly exuberant. Act like an adult. He'll like that, appreciate that, respect that. Colton's easy and calm demeanor had already gotten her to think more as an adult, the way her mother taught her.

Marie knew she had Colton as a boyfriend. But did he see her as a wife? Her heart was overjoyed when she saw him in the schoolyard. She loved surprises. The fact that he had come to town unannounced made her happier than the trip alone would explain. Marie was beyond ecstatic. The man she loved had surprised her with the gift that meant the most--himself, and she hugged his arm as they drove to a small bookstore in the center of town that served coffee and soft drinks in the back of the store.

They ordered sodas and held hands across a table like two teenagers who had never before touched the opposite sex.

"I took a few days off," he said. "I couldn't wait any longer to see you again,"

More sincere words were never spoken, and

Marie gazed with trusting eyes at his handsome, masculine face. "I can stay around until Sunday night. What would you like to do?"

"We could go to your motel, and you could hold me all weekend," she said.

Her words snapped a picture in his mind. They sounded so innocent, but the image that flashed in his brain depicted a situation he did not want. She was not a married woman who he'd never see again or some thirty-something party girl looking for a one-night stand.

Coton knew her body was pleading to be taken-- taken under his with the heat and passion of becoming one, and already, she may have accepted the passion of a boy in town. If so, he would never hold that against her. But for him, he would not do it. She was his darling, his valuable companion, his love. He would not take her to a place where she would grow up before her time. He wanted her innocent smile, her laughing eyes, her sweet endearments. There was time enough to take her into the world of womanhood.

"We could go back to Austin tomorrow night," he said.

"If you like."

"Maybe I should see your father."

Immediately, Marie shook her head. "I don't think that's a good idea. Every time he thinks of you, I get a barrage of questions."

"Can't be that bad, angel. He wants to make sure you're safe."

"No, it's more than that. When I took you and your dad to see mom's grave, I told him about it because he was home when I got back, and asked where I'd been. We began seeing each other at the same time. He's put two and two together."

"So?"

"Something has got him thinking your father's communicated with mom ever since they were in college. It's already an obsession that's as bad a your dad carrying a torch for her all those years."

"What's that got to do with us?"

"Colton, listen to me. My dad must never know who your father is. He will hate you forever, and probably disown me."

"Can't be as bad as all that."

Colton, please. Oh but, if you ever do talk to him, and he asks about strawberries, tell him I fed you and your dad some before we went to the cemetery."

"What?"

"It's a long story. Just tell him you ate the strawberries." She tried to smile.

A terrific crash reverberated through the bookstore like a sonic boom. One wall crumbled partially. Books fell from the shelves in a cascade of thuds. Colton and Marie jumped from their seats and ran out the front door.

A five-ton construction truck, parked on an inclined street, the parking brake failed and the giant vehicle rolled across Spinler's Main Street, miraculously killing no one, took out a standing mailbox and stop sign, and smashed into a garment store. Plate glass shattered across the sidewalk. The truck blocked entry into the garment store, and broke through the interior wall into the bookstore.

Colton could smell gasoline. He sprinted to the back of the building. The backdoor was locked. He yanked on it, kicked, it, but the door held firm. He ran back to the front. He heard terrified screams from within the store. "I've got to go in," he yelled toward Marie. Without waiting another moment, Colton crawled across broken glass, slipped under the truck and around the back tires, and came out in the middle of the store.

A middle-aged woman was pinned between the sales counter and the wall. He pulled at the counter. It wouldn't budge. Daniel ran to the back to find a tool--something--anything to bust up the counter and free the woman. He found nothing but dress racks and clothes hangers. With his bare hands he tore apart a display rack, and ran back to the woman. As soon as he tried to pry the counter apart the rod bent. It was made of aluminum and useless.

Colton turned his back to the counter, and kicked it with all his might. The sideboard split a fraction. With several more kicks the sideboard broke away. The woman remained trapped by the counter, the wall, and the truck. The counter was the only thing he could possibly move. Then, the most horrific condition the two of them could possibly face--the gasoline pool on the floor erupted in flames.

The front of the store quickly became a wall of fire. Garments incinerated like crepe paper. The building interior grew hotter and hotter with each passing second. Smoke billowed against the ceiling, and rolled down the walls. Colton had but seconds to save the woman and himself. He pulled on one end of the counter. The woman screamed as

Colton's force put more pressure on the other end of the counter, but he had no choice. He pried enough space to get behind the counter, and with his back against the wall forced the counter forward. Colton grabbed the woman by the arm and pulled her free. They were both already choking on smoke.

With two hands under her arms he pulled her to the back of the store. High pressure streams of water now sprayed into the front of the store, but it did nothing to help them breathe. He threw his weight against the back door, but it didn't budge.

With all the fabrics and dresses in the store, flames rushed to the back of the building as fast as a firestorm. Colton could no longer see, but by feel, he pulled the woman into the bathroom. There, he doused both of them with water until they were soaked. He saw a tiny sliver of light through a vent in the outer wall, and pried it completely open with the handle from a mop bucket. That gave them some, but very little, fresh air. Colton stood on the toilet, and screamed out the vent opening. "Help! Help!"

The door to the bathroom was now too hot to touch. The woman lay prostrate on the bathroom floor. The heat became oppressive. Colton felt like he was beginning to cook. He screamed out the vent opening for help again and again until he passed out.

CHAPTER TWELVE

Colton woke up on his stomach with 2nd degree burns on his neck, shoulders, and back. Marie was at his bedside when he awoke.

"How do you feel, sweetheart?"

"Uhm, uhm," was all he could utter.

She kissed him on the cheek, and took hold of his hand. It wouldn't have mattered to her if he'd saved a dozen people from a flash flood or a kitten stuck in a tree, Colton was her hero. Dorothy Simmons would never have made it out alive without Colton's heroics. She was a mother of three with a farmer husband. The clothing store was her baby, and had been in operation nearly ten years.

Colton's back was covered with cold, damp cloths. He remained weak and semi-coherent for three additional days due to the pain medicine he'd been given. He could eat sitting up and go to the restroom with help, but the rest of the time he was on his stomach with a pillow under his chest and another under his head.

Marie never even considered going back to class while Colton was in the hospital. The newspaper ran a front page story with pictures of the runaway truck and crushed building. Dorothy Simmons had a broken foot and lacerations to the left side of her body. Her burns were minor compared to Coltons, and she would survive. The entire Simmons family came to visit Colton every other day in the hospital.

His hospital stay ran into a second week, and together, they moved his head down to the other end where, with two pillows under his chest, he could easily look over the foot board. Marie scooted up a chair and they were face to face, talking and smiling, their noses often no more than four inches apart.

"I have something special for you, babe."

"You do?"

"Look here." He pulled out a small black box from the pocket in his gown. "As a token of my affection for you. High school girls like promise rings, don't they? For you, a promise brooch."

He opened the box and she sighed. "Oh Colton. It's so pretty."

She took from the box a brooch about the size of a quarter with a pink opal in the center surrounded by a circle of silver petals. "Colton, it's lovely."

"Well, there's a story behind this. I think this brooch was always meant for you. You see, this brooch was actually given to your mother. When my dad and your mom were dating in college, she took him to a wedding of a close friend. Your mother was the maid of honor. The bride gave all her attendants one of these brooches. Your mom gave it to my dad for safekeeping, and they both forgot all about it. Do you know a Cynthia?"

Marie smiled. "Yes, I know Cynthia. I think her and her family moved to El Paso so I haven't seen her for a long time, but she and mom were very close.

"Well, my dad gave it to me before he went to the big house along with all his keys, and his important papers. But when I saw the brooch and heard the story, I knew who was going to get it. Do I get a kiss?"

Marie said not a word, but leaned in with a tender kiss.

"Keep it with you always."

"I will Colton, I will. You're so thoughtful. I'm so happy your dad passed it on to you." Marie looked the brooch over a moment longer then pinned it to her blouse on the left side over her heart.

A few days later, while Marie was reading her biology book, Colton whispered to her. "Why did I eat the strawberries?"

Marie looked up and her eyes immediately filled with tears. "You are feeling better today."

"Last night," he said, "I dreamt I had an angel by my side. How could I not feel better?"

Marie rubbed the back of her hand across his cheek.

"You can go back to school now. Let me get to know the nurses better."

A laugh sputtered from her thankful expression and she kissed his face. "I love you, Colton King. I will always love you."

CHAPTER THIRTEEN

A ll was not well in the Rucker household. The incident downtown was all everyone talked about. Damage to the building and businesses was estimated at a million dollars. The newspaper had six photos of the scene, and in one of them, Marie stood anxiously at the street corner as firemen strung out their hoses.

The garment shop owner, Dorothy Simmons, had been trapped, and was rescued by a man named Colton King. Robert continued reading. The newspaper went on to state, 'Mr. King is not a local, but he certainly was in the right place at the right time.' Robert finished reading the article, and folded the paper in his lap. Then, like the sun breaking through the clouds, a word flashed in his mind, and he remembered a name from long, long ago--King.

Margie's obsessive college boyfriend was named King--Daniel King. Could this person be related? The paper said he was in the hospital with severe burns. Marie had been coy and quiet when at home the last few days, but gone from the house for longer than school would require.

Robert got in his truck immediately and drove to the hospital. He asked for and received King's room number, and walked down the corridor, curious and tense.

If Marie was there, he would have his answer. Not every answer, but enough to know his intuition was spot on. This man would have been one of the men who came to the house to see Margie, and when they learned she had passed, Marie had taken them to the cemetery. Now, his daughter had fallen for a young man who was only interesting because he wasn't a classmate. Robert shook his head. Unbelievable that his daughter could fall for a complete and total stranger without any knowledge of his family or personal history. Part of him prayed that Marie would not be in the hospital room. But either way, he would find out more about this man named King. It was Daniel King that Robert wanted to beat to a pulp for interfering with his wife's affection and attention. If this man was related, maybe Robert could corner his quarry sooner than later.

Robert slowly opened the nine-foot-high oak door with the huge brass handle. An attendant was ready to leave the room with a meal tray. As the aide passed, there was Marie sitting beside the bed.

Robert did nothing to alarm the patient. His facial expression gained a flicker of amusement and his eyes brightened warmly as though he were especially delighted to see her there.

"How's our hometown hero doing?" he asked.

Marie was speechless. Her face registered total astonishment.

"Well, don't leave me guessing, darling. How's our young man doing?"

"Colton couldn't see, but he could hear. "I'm doing much better, thank you."

"Mind if I sit down?" Robert sat in another chair before she had time to answer. "Tell me, Marie, what's the prognosis?"

"Oh daddy, I'm just visiting. I was downtown when this all happened. I heard the truck crash into the store. This man is a true hero."

"Everyone seems to think so." Robert's mannerisms were so measured and deliberate they gave Marie the chills, and his face wore a demented smirk more than an expression of real caring.

"So how long you going to be laid up, big fellow?"

Colton had been listening intently. He now knew who had entered the room. "Not real sure," Colton said. "All depends on how fast my body heals."

"He's the fella that took you to Austin, isn't he, Marie?"

She didn't have to answer. "And to Dallas at Thanksgiving? My, my. And here you are again. Talk about perfect timing, I mean, Dorothy Simmons is sure glad you like to travel around so much."

Marie found her tongue. "Daddy, you know I've been seeing, Colton. He happens to be very nice to me, and everyone he meets. You needn't come in here with a bunch of vague insinuations. Colton happens to be a perfect gentleman."

Robert ignored her vote of approval. "You never mentioned his last name though, Marie. I saw it in the paper. Front page news. Of course, something like what happened would be. Mr. King, I read. A rather memorable name if I do say. Can't say that I know anyone else with that for a last name." Robert stood. "Anyway, I just wanted to wish you a speedy recovery. I'll see you back at the house. Marie," and he rubbed his thumb across her cheek.

Once in his truck, Robert was immediately on his phone. Robert had no brothers or sisters being an only child, but he had in-laws. He called Margie's eldest brother, Marie's uncle, Rob Winters who worked the old family farm fifteen miles outside of San Angelo.

"Rob, this is Robert. I need your help."

"Sure, what's going on?"

"Marie's having a hard time with her mother's death. She's skipping school. Went on a date with a biker wanna-be, damn guy had a tattoo on his neck. I understand because her and her mother were so close, but she's started arguing with me over every little thing. I'm already at my wits end. Can you take her in for a while? She needs a change of scenery. A farm would be perfect for a month or two. I'll pay you. I don't want her turning suicidal or something."

"Yeah, Margie's death has been hard on us all," Rob said. Margie was his little sister. "But sure, Marie can stay here as long as needed. I'll put her to work feeding chickens and riding a horse. Getting on a horse can be great therapy for sadness."

"Thanks, Rob. I really appreciate it. I'll bring her out this weekend if it's okay?"

"This weekend will be fine."

Robert made the call on a Thursday. Friday evening he told Marie of his plan to drive to San Angelo. "Marie, I'm going to see Grandma Rucker tomorrow, and I'd like you to come along. Being alone, she needs visitors. It would be a change of pace for both of you. We'll be back Sunday afternoon."

"Tomorrow?"

"You know how much she likes to see you. Older folks living alone need company."

"I'd rather stay here. I'll write Grandma a card."

"Marie, I called the hospital. Colton will not be released until next Wednesday at the earliest. If you'll visit Grandma with me, I'll let you drive your friend back to Dallas when he's healthy. You can ride the bus back to Spinler." Marie's body language appeared a bit more cooperative.

"Colton is just resting now. Burns take a lot of time to heal. We can go by the hospital in the morning on our way out of town. Okay?"

Marie nodded. "Okay."

CHAPTER FOURTEEN

N ow fifty years of age, Rob Winters was ten years older than his little sister Margie. He pastured cattle and boarded horses. He loved living on the land, his boyhood home. His wife, Bonnie, was a West Texas girl, born and bred. They had two daughters, both now grown and out of the home. On Saturday, Robert and Marie visited his mother in town, and stayed the night. Sunday morning, they headed out to the farm.

Marie paid no attention when they set out, and was surprised when they pulled up in front of the familiar farmhouse.

"Going to say hello to Rob and Aunt Bonnie?" The statement sounded like a question, but Marie was already confused. Why hadn't her dad mentioned this stop? And while she was mulling over being kept in the dark, Robert opened the club door, opened her backpack, and took out her phone. "You won't need this for a while."

"No, give me my phone."

Robert grabbed her backpack and another small bag, and headed for the farmhouse door.

Bonnie had it open before Robert reached the porch. "Welcome, welcome. I made some fresh cinnamon rolls." Robert followed her into the house. Neither Rob nor Bonnie had much common ground with Robert, but when it came to Margie or Marie, they were as helpful as they could be.

"Is our little princess coming in?" Bonnie asked as Marie sat defiantly in the truck.

"I imagine she'll come in shortly," Robert replied. "We stopped by my mother's last night. Other than that, Marie has been unruly the entire trip, to say the least."

He shook hands with Rob. "I didn't tell her she was here to stay for a while. If I had, I'd never have gotten her in the truck. She graduates in May, but her grades are enough to get her through. Hopefully, she'll be back to her old self long before then, and she can participate in her graduation ceremony."

The three adults sat down to a snack of cinnamon rolls, and milk when the door opened and Marie appeared.

"Would you like a snack?" Bonnie asked as she got up, and hugged her niece. "You look beautiful as always, princess," They walked to the table. "Help yourself."

Marie poured herself a glass of milk, and stood against the kitchen wall. She remained as mute as a mime with a facial expression layered with questions, and a steady gaze ready to kill.

"Sit with us, Marie," Rob said. "We're all family. You'll like it here."

"What!" Milk spewed from her mouth. "What did you say?"

Rob stood and faced her. Tall and lean in Western boots, he was weathered but fit, fully evidenced by his callused hands and deeply tanned face. "You're going to stay with us a while."

"What? No! I have to finish school."

Rob turned and gave his 'help me out here' look at Bonnie. "Look honey," Bonnie said, as she rose from the table. "It's just for a short time. Your mother's untimely passing has been hard on everyone. Your mother was a jewel."

"What are you talking about? My mother was everything to me, and I cried for a week." She stared at the three adults. She saw her father pursing his lips, trying to fade into the wallpaper.

"But I'm not depressed, and I don't go to the cemetery everyday to pine over her grave."

"Sudden tragedies can affect people in different ways," Bonnie said. "You can ride our horses. You like that. Just call it a spring break."

"No!" She glanced at her father again, and he looked as guilty as a cat with feathers in it's mouth. "What has he been telling you?" If her eyes had been lasers, her father would have two holes in his face.

"Just that you need a break, and a change of pace," Bonnie replied.

"That's a lie." Marie was almost screaming now. "He wants--he wants to keep me away from my new boyfriend."

"Come, come, dear. Surely if he's a good young man, he'll still be there for you when you get back home."

Marie threw her glass on the floor, and it shattered across the room. "Are you people deaf?"

Hey, hey, Marie. We'll have no more of that," Rob said. "Do that again and you'll be sleeping in the barn with the dogs and cats. Bonnie show her a room."

Marie was exhausted. She had been sobbing through her verbal tirade, and she let her aunt escort her to the back of the house.

"I better go," Robert said. He gave Rob $400. "Thank you so much. I'll keep in touch. I know this place will do her good."

CHAPTER FIFTEEN

Marie cried as she looked around at what had been her mother's childhood bedroom. She had been to the farmhouse many times before. But now, her father had kidnapped her. Her opinion of his benign, aloof presence in her life had become one of pure hatred. She despised him beyond measure. His scheme to keep her away from Colton would not succeed.

As her sobs dissipated, she immediately realized her behavior would have to be one of obedience and cooperation with her aunt and uncle. Her erratic and boisterous actions upon arrival probably had Rob and Bonnie believing all of her father's lies. Heaven only knew what he had told them. She knew, that for the moment, she was stranded. She could only escape if she won her relatives' trust.

Marie's quickly pitched in with chores around the farm. The place had at least six cats, she wasn't sure exactly, and two Labradors. She quickly made friends with them all. Two weeks into her captivity,

Rob showed her how to saddle a horse. The next day he showed her again. She stood on a step stool to be high enough to throw the blanket in the horse's back. The saddle proved to be a struggle, but she got it done.

The farm was truly serene, far from the incessant rumble of city traffic, away from the almost frantic pace of urban life. The sky was high and blue, so clean you felt you could reach up and touch the clouds. The evening breeze, was cool and soft, a sensation of nature rarely experienced by those living in town. There were smells and sounds bestowed by Mother Nature, completely unfiltered, a direct connection with the land--barrels of hay, whiney of horses, freshly plowed earth, clucking chickens, and the overwhelming scent of approaching rain or the sudden chill that engulfs one's whole body as a cold front passes through.

But despite it's beauty and picturesqueness, for Marie, the farm was an anathema. She would never end her struggle to be reunited with Colton, and every day she schemed different ways she might make her escape. Colton was certainly out of the hospital by now. He had probably looked for her, listened to her dad tell him some lie, and went back to Dallas for the time being.

Rob and Bonnie were seldom gone from the house at the same time. Bonnie made trips to town for groceries and supplies no more than once a week. Rob worked constantly around the farm, and that was Marie's problem--he was always close by.

Her first effort was to mail a letter. Rob and Bonnie thought she was 'improving.' Every week they watched her less and less. After scrounging through drawers around the house, Marie finally found a small 3 X 5 envelope in the dining room bureau. She went to her room and addressed it, and wrote a letter on a napkin.

My dearest Colton,
I'm being held against my will at a farm outside of San Angelo. My father brought me here and lied to my aunt and uncle. Please come and get me. I love you forever. Marie
4899 County Road 853
San Angelo, Texas

Now, she needed a stamp. Rob had his little office in a room behind the kitchen off the same hallway to the garage. Certainly, Rob had to write letters, at least occasionally. One day, when Bonnie was out, Marie slipped into the office. There were two desks on either side of the room. One was covered with papers, but the drawers were virtually empty. The other desk held two monitors for his PC. All the drawers on the right side were locked. But the middle drawer was open, and she hit pay dirt. There was a roll of first class stamps emblazoned with the Stars and Stripes. She tore off three stamps, and quickly slipped from the room.

Now–one more obstacle to overcome. From her bedroom window, she could see the county road in front of the house, and the mailbox. The mail came early every morning, usually before nine. If there was outgoing mail, her observations were that Rob put it out early the same morning when he began his morning routine. She couldn't put her letter out during the night as Rob would see it, and she couldn't put it out after Rob went to the mailbox because there was too little time before the mail truck came by.

She had to put the letter in the box on a day when there was no outgoing mail, and leave the red flag down. Hopefully, the mailman would take it. But she had no way of knowing when either Rob or Bonnie had outgoing mail. She began getting up early when Rob did. She volunteered to feed the dogs, cats, and chickens. Rob was appreciative.

If Rob didn't have a letter to mail, he went out through the garage. If he did, he went out the front door. But the letters would appear from anywhere. He'd grab them from his office desk, a dining room drawer, on top of the microwave. And just because she saw an outgoing letter didn't mean it was going out that day.

She had to take a chance. She slipped out of the house at two in the morning, and placed her letter in the box.

Under a single light in the barn, Rob tended to a newborn calf that was having troubles. He caught a glimpse of someone walking to the road, and he knew it wasn't Bonnie. When he finished in the barn, he walked to the road and looked around. He checked the mailbox, and withdrew a single letter that he stuck in his back pocket. He had had a very long, tiring day. He showered downstairs and went to bed, the letter in his pocket the furthest thing from his mind.

Every night Marie prayed that it would only be a

matter of days before Colton's shiny blue Ram King Cab would pull into the drive, and rescue her. After five days she was beside herself with worry. Doubt shaded in anxiety diminished her hope that was as real as a bird flying from her window never to return. Why hadn't her love come? She feared for Colton's health and safety, and cried for herself.

Had his burn recovery taken a setback? Had he even received the letter? Had he received the letter but decided not to come? Her heart told her this was not true. But the uncertainty that toyed with her thoughts had her in perpetual tears, and she struggled to act normal around her aunt and uncle.

Maybe if she spoke with Rob and Bonnie in a dignified, adult way they might realize she had been brought to the farm under pretense and without justification. They were good people, relatives she adored when she was younger. Trips to the farm were excursions to be looked forward to. Marie knew Rob and Bonnie thought exactly alike. Each of them would have to be convinced for there to be a change in her situation. They had raised two girls themselves. Having seen it before, maybe they thought she was going through a young adult crisis, and took her father's word as gospel, because they didn't have time to psychoanalyze their niece. After all, Rob and Bonnie were busy people. They ran a multi-million-dollar farm. Deep inside Marie knew, she was stuck until her father came for her. If she wanted to escape this rural, windswept prison, she would have to do it on her own.

CHAPTER SIXTEEN

After a seventeen-day hospital stay, Colton was released with celebrity fanfare from the doctors and staff. Long before that, however, he increasingly wondered why Marie hadn't returned to his room. Surely, she and her father were back from their San Angelo trip. Did some school commitments intercede? Even if that were the case, she would have called. There was no answer when he called her, and Colton didn't know her father's number.

As he was wheeled from the hospital, he was greeted by a corridor of colored balloons along the sidewalk. Dozens of townspeople had come out to wish him well. Colton was truly impressed and appreciative. He waved at the gathering as though he were in a parade, and was helped into Morgan's car.

Both Melissa and Morgan had come to Spinler the night before. Melissa would drive him back to Dallas so he could lie down in the backseat, and Morgan would return in his truck.

"Before we leave town," Colton said to Melissa, "I want to make one stop--Marie's house. I haven't seen her for four days and that's not like her."

"I guess not," Melissa grinned, "the way you two were carrying on at Thanksgiving."

"She may have had to tend to something else. She said she was going out of town to see her grandmother. Maybe the woman is ill or something. I don't know. Turn left at the sign. Just say you're a classmate of hers, and you hadn't seen her at school lately."

"Will do." Melissa's knock was answered, and she was in conversation for several minutes at the front door. Colton could see out the side window. Melissa was talking to Mr. Rucker. When she returned to the car, Melissa had little to say.

"He said she's on a school field trip."

"Where to?"

"He didn't say."

"Then when will she be back?"

"This weekend, I think. He was really curt. He didn't elaborate about anything."

"Did you believe him?"

Melissa shrugged her shoulders.

"Damn, I wish I could get up and around. Okay, let's head back, but as soon as I'm well, I'll be back. And when I am, I better find Marie or I'll loosen Mr. Rucker's tongue."

Back in Dallas, the next day, Melissa wrote to her father in jail. She knew his days had to be filled with boredom. He could read, of course, possibly watch TV, and what else? --think about what he'd done. His family was still coming to grips with his conviction. Three to five years wasn't eternity, but time can pass quite slowly when you're behind bars. Despite all of this, Melissa wanted her letters to be upbeat, and filled with positive news. For Melissa, her sadness was draining, but for her father locked up in Huntsville, she would pen fairytales.

Dear Daddy,

We all miss you, but we know you won't be gone long. Mom is back at the pizza shop. She told me last night how much she enjoyed being back there. A change of pace can do anyone some good. With all of us kids grown, I can see it's good for her to get out of the house, and every night we have leftover pizza.

She wants you home. She misses you more than you can imagine, but don't be anxious. The time will soon arrive when you're back. Mom, I'm sure, will bake you a super large, double hand tossed, supreme pizza. Fun!

The school year will soon be over, but all is going well. My grades are very good, and I practice my clarinet every day. I got the non-speaking part of a nurse in the school spring play. The seniors and juniors got all the good parts, but rehearsals have been fun.

Morgan is dating a new guy, a sharp dresser who is majoring in computer science. Her smile is different when she talks about him. Revealing, I'd say. She's had him over several times. Very pleasant and good looking. You may have a son-in-law soon. I think if anything comes of their relationship they'll wait until they graduate, and you'll have plenty of time to witness it.

Colton has been super sweet, as always. He comes over at least once a week, but if mom needs anything special he comes over as soon as he can.

Bye for now. I love you, daddy. Melissa

Melissa blotted her eyes with a tissue lest her tears soil the letter. That was all of the fanciful lies she could come up with today, so she addressed the envelope, and readied it for the mail.

CHAPTER SEVENTEEN

Marie continued doing farm chores with the mind-numbing repetitiveness of a hired hand. She didn't watch TV and ate as often as possible by herself. Sitting with Rob and Bonnie at the dinner table were gatherings of silent tension. Apparently, the two of them had nothing to say to Marie. Marie's inclination toward conversation was similarly nil.

Rob did compliment her on how well she was riding her mare. The praise got Marie thinking. Could she escape the farm on horseback? The thought immediately brought a smile to her brain. The idea was ludicrous. No way could she ride across the countryside to San Angelo, too many fences along the way. She would have to keep to ditches along the highway whenever traffic drove by, and who knew what kind of holes and debris lurked in ravines along the road. Besides, where would she put the horse, if she ever reached town? There was nowhere to put the animal that wouldn't subject it to being injured or stolen.

Marie went to her room, and stared at the ceiling. The idea of making a run for it on the four-wheeler found traction in her thinking, and thereafter held a prominent position in her planning. The machine could do fifty miles per hour without being unstable, would arrive in town much faster than a horse, and she cared nothing about what happened to the machine once she reached town.

It seldom snowed this far south in Texas, but nights could still be quite cold in March. She would have to bundle up when she made her move, which would consist mainly of her work clothes, gloves, and a cap with ear flaps. But her biggest problem was a lack of money. To get a one-way ticket to Dallas, and enough extra for food, she figured she needed at least a hundred bucks. She had managed to pilfer $43 from Bonnie's purse over the many weeks she'd been held at the farm. Marie was pleased when Bonnie had a wad of bills in her purse. A few ones or a five wouldn't be missed. If the purse held only a few bills at any time, Marie put the purse back without taking a thing.

Tomorrow she would make her move. After she rode her horse in the evening, she would brush her down, give her oats, fill her water bucket, and take the keys from the four-wheeler nearest the barn walkway. She had only fifty dollars in cash, but she was ready to make a run for it. She had to try. At 2am, Marie dressed warmly. She raised the blinds and reached for the handle to raise the window sash. Nothing moved. She tried again. It was more than stuck. It was nailed shut.

Marie stepped to her bedroom door and peeked down the hallway. A single amber light in the shape of a flame dimly illuminated the hallway. When Marie reached the darkness of the living room, a lamp came on. Bonnie had been dozing, but she was now fully awake.

"Those clothes look pretty heavy to be sleeping in, Marie."

Marie turned on her heel, already in shock and tears, and rushed back to her bedroom. She threw her coat and other clothes into a pile, and buried her head in her pillow. She bit into her pillow with the ripping ferocity of a pit bull, but her heart was numb and sad. Her aunt and uncle were holding her against her will, and she knew it was completely illegal. For a moment, she wanted to kill them. She would have to kill Rob first, but even then, Bonnie could easily subdue her if they were one on one. Killing them both at the same time might be possible, but she had seen no guns, though Marie was sure there were some around.

Marie said nothing to her aunt and uncle for days after that. The two sides were playing a silent game of cat and mouse. But if her relatives thought they were wearing her down, they were badly mistaken. Marie would find a way to escape the farm even if she had to crawl on her hands and knees all the way to San Angelo.

Marie had two more stamps and another letter already written. She knew the name of the business where Colton worked and that it was on Royal Lane in Dallas. With the letter addressed as best she could, she waited and watched until she could get to the mailbox unseen. One day, Bonnie left early, and Rob was in the field. She rushed the letter to the mailbox before the postman came. Within the half-hour the mail truck came by. Now she knew for certain her letter had gone out.

She had been at the farm for over two months with April just around the corner. She knew Colton was searching for her, but her father would be his only lead. Her father would be full of lies. If he told Colton anything, it would be the misdirection of a totally fabricated story. She knew escape was up to her.

But waiting on a letter to produce results was as stressful as walking a tightrope between two high-rise buildings. The wait was excruciating. After a week, her anxiety turned to depression. She knew it was always possible the letter never made it into Colton's hands, but a cruel voice in the back of her mind kept whispering, 'He's gone. He's forgotten about you. He's on to other women.'

Of course, the easiest way to get to town would be to take either Rob or Bonnie's car. If she could accomplish that, she could theoretically drive all the way to Dallas. But she knew, she'd be pulled over before she ever got that far. And yet, if they were both out of commission, there would be no one around to report a stolen vehicle.

Marie slipped into the master bedroom, took a quick look in the closets, then checked the night stands. When she opened the second drawer, there it was--a short barrel handgun. She had no idea of the caliber and didn't care. She saw the lever just above the trigger. It was easily touched by a person's thumb when held in the right hand. She assumed it was the safety and clicked it up and down. Marie slipped out of the bedroom as fast as she could.

She would shoot her aunt and uncle one at a time when they entered the house. In her room, down beside her bed, she pulled back the carriage, and a bullet ejected. She let the bolt snap back into place. The gun was loaded.

She remembered when she was a little girl, and Uncle Rob had put her on the back of a horse and she clung to his belt loops for a ride around their arena. But today, she was almost nineteen. She was being restrained against her will all because her father didn't want her to see the man she fully intended to marry. For a few hundred dollars a month, and a fabricated story from her despicable father, her aunt and uncle possibly thought they had her all figured out, with all her escape routes blocked. They didn't even know what was about to hit them.

Around noon, Rob came in the house.

"Can I get you anything?" Marie asked as Rob washed his hands at the sink by the back door.

"A tall glass of iced tea would be nice. I can fix myself a sandwich."

Marie poured the tea, set the glass on the table, and went to her room. There she waited several minutes for him to make himself a sandwich, and sit at the table.

When she poked her head around the hallway door, Rob had his back to her. The gun was in her hand. The safety was off. She knew it was loaded. Marie stepped into the living room, and gazed at the fifteen feet between her and her uncle. The air in the room suddenly became stifling, hotter and oppressive as if it were choked with dust. She wanted to cough, but dared not. Sweat drenched her scalp, and the weight of the gun became as heavy as an anvil in her grip.

Her gaze fixated on the back of her uncle's head. She needn't take another step. She could shoot him from where she stood. Whether it was sweat or tears, a waterfall quickly obscured her vision, and she had to turn away. She walked softly back to her room and fell across her bed. It wasn't for lack of resolve that she cried. She knew deep down inside she could never shoot someone, certainly not her mother's brother and his wife. She cried because, once again, she knew she was still trapped. Trapped: what a terrible, heartless word. And the most horrible thought of all--she had no idea when it all might end.

CHAPTER EIGHTEEN

C olton remained around the house for the last few days of his recovery. His employer already knew the story. Colton had sent the company a copy of the Spinler newspaper that chronicled the entire event of the unoccupied construction truck that had plowed into a Main Street building. He spent time with his mother, holding her hand, and talking to her even though she appeared asleep. If she knew he'd been injured or in the hospital, she gave no acknowledgment.

With Daniel's incarceration, Brenda became totally despondent and withdrawn. Her children's efforts to snap her from her lethargy failed completely. When a person fully realizes the deception they've lived with, the bonds of trust that was never there, where half-truths and manipulation were the order of the day rather than honest discussions, it can crack a soul as easily as snapping a dried twig.

Brenda's personal hygiene suffered. When she infrequently walked about, she smelled like a hamper of mildewed clothes. Within a month, she never left the bed. Melissa had to feed her, and help her to the bathroom. The light in Brenda's mind had been extinguished. For now at least, the black cloud deep within her eyes gave testimony that her brain sought refuge and safety. The children's efforts to snap her out of it were fruitless, because at Brenda's home address--there was no one there.

Colton hadn't seen or heard from Marie in nearly two weeks. The burns on his back were healing, but the skin was tender, and any touch other than a cold pack could generate feelings anywhere from unpleasant tingles to shots of excruciating pain. He now knew, calls to her phone were a waste of time. He was done waiting around. Something had happened to Marie, good or bad he didn't know, but he would search until he found her. He knew in his heart she wasn't away from him of her own choice.

Morgan made a cape, of sorts, of white muslin that covered his shoulders to his lower back. She fashioned a collar fastened with Velcro strips. He wore a light cotton shirt over it. He kissed his mother's cheek and hugged the girls, and set off for Spinler once again.

As he drove south, Colton was more worried than upset about Marie's disappearance. He had reason to distrust her father. Marie's cautionary note not the least of his apprehensions, but he had no one else to speak to. He would check with the helpful lady at the high school office if there had been a field trip and if, in fact, Marie had been attending classes. Beyond that, had she been injured, had she run away. Colton racked his brain for any reasonable explanation for her absence. He had no answer, because there was none. Marie would not vanish without contacting him. Her touch, her smile, her kiss told him all that had meaning. Her father, Mr. Rucker, knew whatever there was to know. Once he got face to face with the man, Colton would play the polite, concerned boyfriend. Colton still prayed there was a logical explanation for the mystery. But if the older fellow began spewing a bunch of double talk, Colton might make him a candidate for his old hospital room.

It was just after 5pm, when he got to Spinler, and he went straight to the Rucker home. The door was answered after a few knocks. Robert stood on the threshold several inches above him.

"Well, if it isn't our town hero. How are your burns?"

"Tender--but getting better. Thanks for asking. Is Marie home?"

"Not at the moment. Would you like to come in?"

The offer was cordial, still Colton found it odd. "Okay."

Rucker directed him to the living room, a formal area off the den that was seldom used. Colton sat in the same chair in which his father had waited after he snuck into the house. Rucker sat on the edge of the couch.

"So you're the new flame in Marie's heart?"

Colton cleared his throat. "I guess you could put

it that way. Did you say she'd be home soon?"

"Soon enough. Since you stopped by, I thought we'd have a little chat. If this thing between you and her becomes serious, I should get to know you better."

Colton was wary of such a conversation. He didn't know all Marie had told him about the two of them. Although Rucker's voice was relaxed and measured, his eyes had a piercing quality like a hawk circling for prey.

"You met Marie at her mother's funeral. Is that right?"

"Not exactly. My father and I stopped by coming back from deep-sea fishing out of Galveston."

"So he made over a hundred mile detour just to drop by and say hello to Margie?" Colton shrugged his shoulders. "He said she was an old acquaintance. That's all I know."

"So your dad's from San Angelo?"

"I really don't know where he grew up. I'm adopted."

"Humm. Well, tell me. What's your father's name?"

"Michael King. He was quite upset to learn of your wife's passing. I'd like to express my condolences as well. She helped raise a wonderful girl like Marie, I know she was an outstanding woman."

"Yeah… it was all quite a shock," Rucker replied with an inflection in his voice of true sorrow.

"By the way, Mr. Rucker, I'm sorry we ate all of your strawberries. Marie was very sweet and helpful that morning, especially when my dad learned the bad news. She made us fresh coffee, too. At the cemetery we got to talking while my father paid his respects at Mrs. Rucker's grave."

Robert Rucker sat straight up, instantly snapped from his reminiscing. Colton had just tripped up. Rucker might make a cup of instant coffee for himself before he went to work. But neither Margie nor Marie touched the stuff. They didn't even own a coffee pot.

Rucker stood. His face twisted into a fierce expression, his teeth set in a grimace, and his gaze focused in on Colton like a laser.

"Young man, I don't want you seeing my daughter. You've lied to me, and I don't believe any of your story. Now get out."

Colton stood and didn't move an inch. Both men were of equal height, and for a moment, the room went silent.

"Look, old timer, I didn't come here for your permission about anything. Marie is legally an adult, and I know she wants me at her side."

"I said, get out. Marie is not here, and she will never be back. She is gone to you. Go away."

Colton thrust his hands forward and grabbed Rucker by the shirt. Rucker twisted away. His buttoned-down shirt ripped. Colton threw a punch. A quick turn by Rucker, and the fist hit him in the shoulder. As Colton was turned slightly, Rucker yanked his arm, and threw an open-handed slap that caught Colton square in the back.

Colton dropped as though he'd been shot. Every nerve fiber in his body screamed pain. His toes went numb. His ears felt hot. If he were being eaten alive it would have hurt no worse. Rucker could beat him to death right then and there, and Colton would have been unable to raise a finger to stop it. The pain on the entirety of his back felt as though the skin had been ripped from his ribs, and he was so overcome with pain, he could not move.

Rucker went into Colton's pocket, pulled out his cell phone, and stomped it to smithereens with the heel of his boot. "Good grief, you demented hick. You didn't have to do that."

Rucker swung back his leg as though he were about to kick Colton in the chest. "Don't," Colton pleaded. "I'm down, I'm done. Just stop."

Rucker went to the garage, and retrieved a crowbar. At the front door, he jabbed the iron bar against the locking mechanism until the wood was visibly scarred, then threw the bar in the flowerbox. He went to his phone at the kitchen counter and called the police.

When the police showed up, Rucker was ready with his speech.

"This kid broke in my house and accosted me. He tore my shirt and he's been stalking my daughter. He should be charged with breaking and entering and assault. I'm pressing charges."

Colton was still on the floor, but he had sat up. "He's lying. He asked me to come in,"

"Get up," the cop said. "You're coming with me."

"I've got some severe burns on my back. Could you cuff me in front?"

The cop took a second look. "What do you know? The town celebrity breaking into houses.

Talk about a turn of events."

"I didn't break in, officer. And I'm not stalking anyone. He has his daughter sequestered, and I know she wants to see me."

"If you say so. We'll figure this out at the station." He cuffed Colton's hands in front. "Okay, let's go."

Colton was placed in the holding cell at the Spinler police station. The cop that arrested him at the motel the night he first arrived in Spinler was on duty, and recognized Colton immediately. "So what brings you back? You miss me?"

Colton's burned back still stung like being sliced with scalpels. He grabbed the bars, and leaned into the space. "Mr. Robert Rucker has hidden his teenage daughter away, and I know it's against her will. You met her, remember? At the door of the house we went to on Sycamore. When I asked about Marie, he asked me to come in. It was all a ploy so he could start a fight, and claim home invasion and assault. None of it is true."

"Humm. If this Rucker fellow files a complaint, you'll be here at least until morning when you'll see a judge." The cop took a moment to look Colton over. "I believe you. With your reputation in town, I think the judge would set a low bail."

"I've got less than $50 in my wallet, and only a couple of hundred on a debit card. But I have to get out of here. Marie Rucker is my girl, and her old man is not keeping me away from her. What do you think bail will be?"

"I have no idea, but-- I was thinking. I bet you and I together could get Brad Simmons to put up the money. After all, you saved Dorothy's life. It's not that late. I'll give him a call now."

Colton sat on a bunk, and leaned forward to diminish the pain in his back. He never dreamed a few square inches of skin could contain so many volcanic nerves.

"Simmons said he would do it. I'm to call him when I know the time of your arraignment, and he said he'd come straight to the courthouse," the cop said. "But tell me--why does Rucker have it in for you? Most folks around here think you're pretty special. You know not everyone has the guts or the ability to do what you did,"

"It's a family thing. He hates my dad."

"So what's that got to do with you?"

"Exactly. The guy lost his wife a couple months ago, but he's an introverted, control freak. His daughter and I hit it off when we met, and he's determined to keep us apart. I'm telling you, Robert Rucker is a sick man."

"Okay," the cop said. "I'll do all I can to get you out of here as soon as possible. You need to be looking for his daughter. In fact, I'll get a photo of her and send out an APB. The police and sheriff departments all over Texas will know she's missing.

CHAPTER NINETEEN

Heath Diebold continued to haunt the alleys, porn shops, and bars along Harry Hines Blvd. There was always someone around from whom he could bum a smoke or go halves with on a bottle of Ripple. He put in six hours a day at the warehouse, made sure he kept his appointments with his parole officer, and constantly wondered where Morgan, his birth daughter was.

She'd be twenty-one, or maybe twenty-two by now. She could be married. At that age, she may have already left the King's home. Colton would tell him nothing about her. He needed to see her. His memory of a pretty little girl turning from a toddler into a sweet little thing made regular appearances in his dreams. He'd like to strike up a conversation with her. He would have to look and act his best.

If they should meet, he could already see the reaction in her eyes. There would certainly be surprise, a hesitation as she looked him over, a close study of his face. If she were wary, he would understand. The next reaction would convey her state of mind. If her eyes brightened, he knew she would speak with him. If her gaze turned pensive, Heath would ask if she'd sit with him on the porch. She would not fear him in any physical sense, but how curious would she be to know how he'd been doing?

A father should get to see his grown child at least once.

The list of Dallas area residents with the last name of King was entirely too long to tackle. His only option was to go by Colton's place of employment again. Heath got Joe to drive him there, but Colton's truck was not in the parking lot. The two men went by the business twice a day for three additional days, and never saw Colton's truck. Heath had an idea.

He borrowed a phone from a guy who apparently didn't have enough money to buy a razor to cut his scraggly beard, but he had a cell phone. The guy's name was Ralph Stutsman, and with that in mind, Heath made the call.

"All Seasons Heating and Air."

"Hello, my name is Ralph Stutsman and I'm the maintenance man at Colton Kings's residence. He works for you, correct?"

"Yes."

"The reason I'm calling is because his mailbox is overflowing, and when I peeked inside his residence there was food spoiling in the refrigerator. Has he been coming to work?"

"No, no. You haven't heard? He was injured in a fire, and has been in the hospital."

"Oh, that is news. Is he going to be alright?"

"As far as I know, he's supposed to make a full recovery."

"Do you have a contact person for him?"

"I could look and see," the woman said, "but don't you have that kind of information, too."

"Unfortunately, no. That's why I'm calling around. The rent is past due, and we need someone to pick up this mail."

"Just a moment, let me see what we have." A minute later, she was back on the line. He has a Daniel and Brenda King listed. I believe they are his parents, and they live at 5113 Tree Top in Garland. The number I have is 214-762-2463."

"Thank you so much. You've been very helpful. Thanks again."

When Heath got off the phone he was beyond elated. The phone call had been better than sex. Garland was clear on the other side of Dallas from where he was, but he'd walk every step of the way if he had to. He would find the residence at the address of 5113 Tree Top and see Morgan again. Heath could feel it. His daughter was just around the corner, within inches of his grasp.

CHAPTER TWENTY

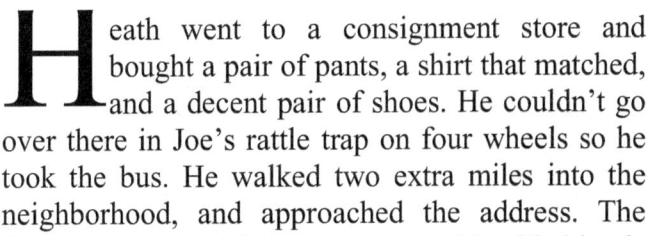

Heath went to a consignment store and bought a pair of pants, a shirt that matched, and a decent pair of shoes. He couldn't go over there in Joe's rattle trap on four wheels so he took the bus. He walked two extra miles into the neighborhood, and approached the address. The door was answered by a teenage girl with blonde hair.

"Good afternoon. Is this the King residence?" Heath tried to appear as friendly as possible, but a smile wasn't in the performance. His chipped and missing teeth were best kept behind tight lips.

"Who wants to know?" The girl was already suspicious, but Heath continued.

"I'm looking for Morgan King. I'm her uncle from Tyler. Just thought I'd say hello if she was around."

"What did you say your name was?"

"I'm sorry I didn't introduce myself. I'm Orval Hicks. I'm her mother's brother."

"Well, I think she's at school," and immediately, Melissa wished she hadn't said a word. It occurred to her that the story always was that Morgan and Colton had been in foster care for three years before her parents had adopted them. Where was this guy during those years? Furthermore, she had never laid eyes on this man in all the years she had lived with her two adopted siblings.

"Will she be home soon? I'm in the oil business. Been in Saudi Arabia the past eight years. I imagine she looks a lot different than when I last saw her."

"I don't know when she'll be back."

"Could I wait here on the porch?"

"Where's your car?"

"Oh, I haven't had a car in years. Flew in last night, took a taxi to the hotel, and a bus out here. I'll be taking a bus back to Tyler, as well. That's why I was hoping to see Morgan before I leave."

What the guy said sounded reasonable, almost rehearsed the way the words flowed from his lips. But Melissa sensed something not quite right, and her fingers slowly went to the handle on the screen door, and made sure it was locked. "Wait here. I'll try to call her."

When she reached Morgan, "There's a man at the house to see you," Melissa said.

"Byron came by? He should have called me."

"No, he's an older guy. He says he's your uncle."

Morgan was ready for news of another sort, and found what she heard puzzling. She had never known relatives of her birth parents. The more she thought, the surer she was. If this guy was her uncle, the only time he had ever seen her was when she was a baby. Yet, Morgan's mental makeup was more curious than suspicious. She was more accommodating than critical.

"I'll head to the house,"she said, and hung up.

Morgan had always been polite, friendly, and approachable. If a person was amazed or jealous of her stunning facial features, Morgan was never condescending or catty. She was reserved which some people took for arrogance. Morgan took it all in stride. She knew she caught men's eyes, and that she was attractive, though she didn't consider herself beautiful. She had no one to defeat or battles to fight.

As she drove to the house, she wondered who had stopped by. If the man was looking for money, he would be sorely disappointed The days of living in a house torn with domestic violence had been years ago. Her antenna to detect duplicitous conmen was rusty with disuse. Twenty-one- year-old Morgan King was a young woman as naive as she was gorgeous. But life has a way, sooner or later, of taking everyone, kicking and screaming, to the school of hard knocks.

As Morgan exited her car at the house, and Heath took two steps off the porch, their meeting seemed to take place in slow motion. Morgan stopped on the pathway as the man approached.

"It's a real pleasure to see you again, Morgan," and he extended his hand.

She shook it politely, but quickly. "You're my mom's brother?"

"Yessirree, little brother that is. There's two years between us. Can we sit on the bench?"

Morgan led the way up the porch steps. All the while, Melissa stood in the doorway.

"This young lady was very helpful when I knocked. Who is she, may I ask?"

"My little sister. I don't remember ever seeing you."

"Oh yes. I saw you many times when you were a toddler. I've been out of the country or I would have tried to see you more often."

"Are you married?"

"Divorced, I'm sad to say. I wish we hadn't split, but what can I say? Keep your chin up, and keep looking to the future with a positive attitude."

Totally without suspicion or judgment, Morgan looked the man over as he spoke. His face was white rather than tan indicative of a recent shave. His hands were beyond rough, his fingernails yellow, and if he was in his mid-forties, the man looked much older than that. Then, from the deepest recesses of her unconscious mind, Morgan's brain retrieved a memory filed away long ago. The man had a brown mole the size of a pea that claimed space on his left earlobe. Morgan remembered playing with that ear as a toddler. The realization widened her eyes. This man was her birth father. Something within her wanted to hug him right then and there. Despite his fabricated stories, she wanted to touch him. No matter what kind of person he was, he was still her father, and the fact that he'd gone to the trouble to come and see her made her giddy.

"Would you like something to drink?" Morgan asked.

"Sure, if it's no trouble."

Melissa went to the fridge for three bottles of water, and the girls listened to his stories for another twenty minutes. Melissa didn't know the tales were most likely lies. Morgan didn't care.

"Would you girls like to go get something to eat? There's an IHOP just down the road."

During the time Heath sat on the porch, his stories flowed like a man recalling great adventures. Upon closer inspection, however, Heath looked more like a grunt in the boiler room than the captain of a great ship. But he had made no fanciful claims. Heath said he worked in the oilfields, subject to the drying, abominable heat of the Arabian desert. His travels to foreign lands set the framework for his exotic tales, not his personal exploits, and Melissa listened patiently, while Morgan dwelt on his every word.

"I'd love to go eat." Morgan said.

"I'd better stay," Melissa said, "in case mother wakes up. She's been a bit under the weather."

"We'll be back in less than an hour," Heath assured her.

At the restaurant, they each ordered pancakes and scrambled eggs..

"Please tell me about my mother." Morgan said." As they ate, Heath told her all the nice things he could think of about Donna, actually his wife, not his sister. He thought about the night Donna's father and two brothers threatened him if he didn't marry the unattractive woman. He had gotten her pregnant with the child that would become Colton. She had already been passed around to other men, and she had no chance of marriage with a kid in tow--so Heath did. Donna's male relatives convinced Heath it was his best course of action..

"So what keeps you busy, Morgan?"

"I'm a senior in college, working toward my degree in elementary education. I love the idea of being a teacher."

Heath reached across the table, and touched her hand.

"It's nice you agreed to visit with me." For a moment they just gazed at one another, and Heath withdrew his hand. "Do you have a job too?"

"I tutor a few high school students in the evening. That's all."

"Really? What do you make from that, if I can ask?"

"About a hundred a week, maybe one-fifty."

Heath was instantly astonished. He made more than that sweeping floors and moving boxes at the warehouse. "That doesn't go very far, does it?"

"No."

"I know where you can make a lot more than that, like $300 to $400 a night, and all you have to do is beam your pretty smile."

Morgan's expression didn't change. Neither did she speak. But her rapt attention gave Heath the permission to continue, and the conniving lobe of his duplicitous brain took hold, and he began to weave another tale.

"It can be hard for anyone to make money when they're young, just getting started That's not fair. The way jobs and money work, a lot of older folks who do very little at work still get to collect their big salaries only because they've been around a long time.

"For someone like you, young and with a pretty face, you can make really good money just posing for pictures. Ever thought of that?"

Morgan shook her head.

"Have you ever heard of strippers? Well, I'm not talking about that at all. Some girls do that though, pole dancing and the like, to make money for college. Know any girls like that?"

Again, Morgan shook her head.

"I don't recommend it. Guys are up close, touching the girls to give them money. I just want to be clear. There are plenty of men who will pay top dollar to see pretty girls, but being touched and such . . ." He shook his head like she would automatically know what he meant.

"I know a nice couple that run a disco club where some of the girls dance behind plexiglass screens. They dance in frilly outfits and make like $50 an hour, but nobody can ever touch them."

Morgan searched his eyes to find the meaning behind his sketchy oratory. "I would like to make some money."

"Well, we could make a quick run over there now, and you could see some of the girls, or we could go back in the morning, and I could introduce you to the owners."

Morgan's mind juggled all she'd heard. Lingering apprehensions nudged her thinking, and the admonitions of the little voice in the back of her brain told her this was something she should probably avoid. But, curiosity pulled at her naivete.

What exactly was 'Uncle Orval' referring to? Maybe it would be easy, rewarding, even exciting. "Give me a minute. I'll call my sister."

When the phone was answered, Morgan said, "We're going downtown. I won't be out long."

Dallas was falling into evening as red and orange clouds colored the horizon to the west, high above DFW International Airport. Harry Hines Blvd. was coming alive, as well. Neon lights flickered on to welcome the coming darkness. The parking lots of bars and gentleman's clubs filled for happy hour.

With Morgan willing to go to his section of town, Heath knew he had a couple of minor problems on his hand. First of all, she was wearing a dress. She was already gorgeous. If any patrons saw her, she'd smell like fresh meat in front of hungry lions. The other girls would immediately hate her. Secondly, he would have to direct her to drive around to the back of the store since a huge sign reading ADULT VIDEO was plastered to the front of the building.

However, he could work through all of that. Heath's only interest was Mike and Ginny Cook, owners of the place, and also his source for internet searches. They would pay him handsomely to get a girl of Morgan's beauty in the lineup. Morgan could do it, shake her butt and show some skin. She would do it. She would want to do it. If not, he would make her do it.

Ginny came out and met Morgan at the car. She was the kind of woman who could take a neophite in the sex trade, and with a gentle touch and soft words show a new girl the ropes like she was teaching her how to knit.

Ginny had one of the girls begin a performance and she, and Morgan took seats in a viewing room. The girl was a leggy blonde with bright blue eyes. As much as patrons wanted to see female bodies, it was the eyes that made the deal. No matter how shapely the body or smooth the skin, sunken, dead eyes never made the cut. Girls whose eyes were void of light and life were shown the door. Then came the smile, and perky breasts, but without the glow of dazzling eyes, the girl never made the stage.

The girl's outfit was full of sequins and tassels. Tiny rhinestones had been pasted over her body.. She danced slowly to a mournful ballad with bends and twists. The girl could even do the splits. At times, she leaned against the glass and pushed her breasts against it. The whole routine wasn't a dance, per se, but a series of seductive gyrations.

Morgan watched in a puzzled trance. Ginny kept whispering to her. When the girl unbuttoned her bra in the front and slowly opened it, Morgan's eyes bulged from her skull. And yet, she didn't move or comment. The girl continued to shake her butt at the audience and make her breasts visible from every angle. When the fourth song ended, the show was over.

Back in the office, Ginny didn't ask her what she thought of the show or if she could see herself doing it. She concentrated on the money.

Morgan, she cooed in her motherly voice, "You do what you just saw, six to eight times a night and you'll easily take home over $200 a night. To do eight performances only requires you to be here for four hours a day. We'll start you tomorrow with no disrobing. All of that will come with time. What hours can you be here?"

Morgan was caught between two friendly lechers, and she didn't know what to say. She felt numb, but not appalled. It did look easy, and semi-anonymous. What were the chances someone she knew would take in a show like the one she just saw? But there was one question that didn't cross her mind, probably the most important question she should have asked herself--what will this lead to? "I'll come in tomorrow at this time. For four hours?"

"Four hours, sweetie. That's what all the other girls work."

CHAPTER TWENTY-ONE

Brad Simmons gladly posted Colton's bond the next day. He returned to his motel to fully rest and recuperate. No more trips back and forth to Dallas. Once he found Marie, he would move to Spinler until she graduated high school. In the meantime, Morgan and Melissa could go to his apartment, collect the mail, give notice of his intention to move, and begin to clear out his unit.

Colton had a room at the Cactus Trail Motel, the same motel where he'd nearly startled the clerk to death when he woke her in the middle of the night, and demanded to know if his father had rented a room. Now, after his downtown heroics, Colton was a celeb all over town, and the Vietnamese women took to him like a movie star. They laughed when recalling events of that night, and now she tended to him like a nurse. For three weeks she assisted him and brought him food. He could take no more chances with his tender back. What burned skin needed most to heal was time. The woman charged him only $100 a week even though she kept herself at his beck and call, and doted on him as though he were one of her own.

Two front office secretaries handled the mail at All Seasons Heating & Air. The woman who talked to Heath when he inquired about Colton's whereabouts, held a letter in her hands. It was sent to Colton, but addressed to the firm. Actually, the letter contained no address besides Colton's name, and the business name at Royal Lane, Dallas, Texas. She could only assume the letter got delivered because the mailman knew the businesses along his route.

She knew of Colton's injury in a fire and the likelihood he was laid up somewhere recuperating. It was probably best not to wait until he returned to work to give him the letter, so she again looked up his emergency contact, and forwarded the letter to Tree Top Lane in Garland.

Both Melissa and Morgan were still in school and attended classes during the day. After classes, Melissa planned to go to Colton's apartment. She wanted Morgan to go with her, but her sister had begun begging off simple errands that would assist their mother or brother. Melissa went by herself and gained access to his mailbox and apartment when she showed the property manager the article about the fire in the Spinler newspaper. Melisssa took a few items easy to carry in the car, and headed back home. Just going through his mail would take time. She knew he'd want to know if anything important had come in.

Melissa was also concerned about the change she saw in Morgan. It was impossible not to notice. Some evenings, she saw Morgan's face when she got home, washed but not clean. The lingering red of ruby lip gloss and turquoise mascara still in the folds of her eyelids told a story Melissa was reluctant to pursue. The gold glitter along her hairline and around her ears was unmistakable, and when she stepped in the shower, Melissa saw tiny rhinestones still pasted to her skin.

On Saturday, they went together to Colton's apartment to begin cleaning out the place.

"So you're a showgirl now?" Melissa asked.

Morgan's personality didn't know the meaning of rude or tacky retorts. In fact, her entire demeanor relaxed, and she sighed as though her whole body had been praying for someone to acknowledge her situation, and she began to cry.

"Oh my gosh, Morgan. What is it?" Melissa immediately pulled the car into a retail strip and parked. "Has somebody hurt you?"

Melissa pulled her sister to her and hugged her. "Go on. Let it out. We're in no hurry." Melissa reached for a box of tissues from the glove box and gave them to her.

It took every bit of five minutes for Morgan to compose herself, and then, with bloodshot eyes and a runny nose, she told a story Melissa thought impossible. Morgan bared her soul, and Melissa knew every word was true.

"That was not my uncle who came to the house. It was my real dad. When we went to town, he showed me a place where girls dance for money. It all sounded so simple. I've made almost two grand in two weeks with tips and all. I wish I hadn't taken a dime."

"You mean you're stripping?"

"Yes, but behind a glass barrier. I thought it sounded so easy."

"What do you do?"

"At first it was just shaking my butt and making eye contact. I knew they wanted me to take off my bra, and for the last four nights, I have. I didn't want to, but the men can't touch you. Oh god, I feel sick." Morgan choked back a sob and caught her breath. "Now they insist I get my crotch all trimmed real dainty like and take off my panties. Oh, Melissa, what can I do?"

"Quit! They're using you. You don't have to put up with that crap."

Morgan slowly shook her head. "I already tried. That man, my own father, is now like a rabid dog. He won't take no for an answer. If I don't show up every afternoon at six, he'll track me down, and beat me up. He knows where we live. You're probably in danger, too.

"No, I don't care. We'll call the cops."

"I don't think you know, but he beat my real mother so hard and often she died. That's why Colton and I were available for adoption.

"Are you supposed to go in tonight?"

"Yes, it's Saturday night. I know I'm the prettiest girl they have. If I don't show my father won't be the only one after me. The place is run by a married couple of losers. The place is nothing but a porn shop. I messed up good this time."

Melissa hugged her again. "I don't care what you think, Morgan. Nobody can make you do something against your will, and not have to answer for it. Those people have you brainwashed. I'm with you in this one hundred percent. Don't go back in. If you don't like it, don't do it."

Morgan tried to smile at Melissa. "I love you, little sis. I should have told you about this days ago. But, I'm going to in tonight. I'm afraid--I'm going to back until Colton gets back in town.

CHAPTER TWENTY-TWO

Days on the farm passed with the interminable crawl of a crippled sloth. The days became warmer as March turned to spring. Marie's senior high class would be graduating in mid-May, and Marie knew she would not be with them. She now had a total of $88, all stolen from Bonnie's purse, and Marie could wait no longer.

After she had ridden her horse that night, she fed the mare, and put her in her stall, Marie didn't go to the house. Wearing only a jacket to ward off the evening chill, she ran to the far end of the property, and took to the ditch beside the road. She would walk the fifteen miles to town.

She would like to hitch a ride, and when she got further down the road, she might give it a try. She had a 4" blade hunting knife with her for protection, but she knew the safety of any ride largely depended upon lady luck. She prayed she might catch a ride with an elderly couple headed to San

Angelo. If she happened to hail a group of young hooligans who saw she was all alone, she would be at their mercy.

The moon was high. The ditch was dry. Each step invigorating rather than tiring. Whenever a vehicle approached, she ducked down until it passed. She decided not to take any chances trying to thumb a ride. She could walk at five miles per hour, at least. At that rate she would be in town in three hours. She pressed on. She would never go back to the farm.

It was just after 9 pm when Marie reached the outskirts of San Angelo. Traffic picked up as she passed a few darkened buildings, but the city's center was only a cluster of tall shapes in the distance. She ran into a man locking a door, and asked for help.

"Can you help me?" she asked.

The man was well dressed in slacks and a dress shirt. He looked her over, and seemed slightly amused. "I'll try. What do you need?"

"I got dropped off out here. My ride headed that way," and she pointed. "I was hoping to get to the bus station."

"Well--that's not the way I'm headed, but it's not that far. I'll give you a ride."

They traveled in silence and Marie was relieved. She didn't have the energy to make up stories on the fly. The driver pulled to the curb at the bus station, and Marie reached for the door handle. "Thanks," she said.

"Hold on just a minute. Don't be in such a hurry. You asked for help. Let's make sure you can get where you're going. Where are you headed?"

Marie sat back. The man sounded genuinely interested in her plight, and he had driven her straight to the depot. "Dallas."

"Do you have the fare?"

"I think so."

"Let's check." He took his phone and requested the ticket price to Dallas. A bus would be leaving at 10:30, headed north to Abilene, then east on I-30 to Dallas. The price was $83. "Do you have eighty-three dollars?" He could tell she was desperate though not frantic. Probably a runaway, but she looked like a schoolgirl simply caught in a bind. He had a wife and a family. He had his own problems and bills to pay. But the goodness that dwells in every heart, though often cloaked in indifference, surfaced, and the man wanted to help her though his kindness would never be repaid nor would he ever see her again.

"Just $88, I think."

"You have to eat, too, don't you?"

The wetness in her eyes shone in the car's dome light as she nodded. Her face was a portrait of hope and vulnerability, and she waited.

The man reached for his wallet and pulled out all the bills. He had a twenty, two fives, and four ones and he gave them all to her.

"Oh, thank you. Thank you so much."

"You're welcome. Take care of yourself.

Marie exited the car wiping tears from her face, and she waved to him as he pulled from the curb and drove off.

The trip to Dallas took all night, with stops at

every dot on the map along the way. With Dallas being a major destination the bus was nearly full, and Marie found herself in a carnival sideshow with no escape. The girl across the aisle had just gotten a cell phone, or a new one at least, and had to call everyone she knew, and talk about nothing well into the night. There was the incessant squalling of infants, and sporadic protests from fussy toddlers. Two guys in the back played a continuous game of Texas Hold'em with snapping cards keeping most awake, and Marie had the bad luck of sitting next to a huge black woman that, even with the armrest raised, took up most of Marie's seat. A powerful swath of body odor was the scent of the day, and Spanish was the primary means of communication. Modern day bus travel was the privy of the unvarnished underclass. Gone were the days where blue-haired grandmothers traveled in comfort and quiet to visit grand children halfway across the country.

Once in Dallas, Marie found a terminal that could best be described as a menagerie of organized chaos. She had no luggage. She stepped off the bus knowing she would quickly garner attention as no one was there to meet her, and she didn't know what to do next. She wanted to leave the depot, but she didn't want to wander down some dead-end street. She wanted to call Colton, and knew his address, but she had neither a phone nor was she sure she had enough for taxi fare. She didn't want to head his way until she first talked to him, anyway. She hadn't eaten anything at their stops throughout the night.

As dawn crept above the skyline, she stepped outside, and was immediately engaged in conversation by a young man who made her feel creepy from the moment he said hello.

"If your ride is taking you north, I've got ten bucks I can pay if you'd give me a lift," he said.

Marie looked back at him with benign revulsion. She didn't want to piss him off, but neither did she want to act friendly. "We'll be headed south," she said.

"You live in Oak Cliff or Duncanville? Maybe Lancaster?" The hustler read her like a picture book, and he knew, she didn't know up from down in the big city.

"Does it matter? The bus ran late, I was told."

"Just trying to help."

"Help? You said you needed a ride."

"Let's just say you looked like you could use some help."

"Do you have a phone?"

"Matter of fact, I do."

"Can I make a call?"

The young man handed her the phone. He'd been down this road before. If she reached who she was looking for, he'd leave her alone. Someone would be expecting her--and looking for her. On the other hand, if she didn't reach anyone, he'd lay on the charm. His assistance would be in demand. He would play out a well-rehearsed plan of action.

Her face became more troubled with each passing ring, and when she spoke he knew the number had gone to voicemail.

"Colton, I'm here in town at the bus station. I

thought you'd be waiting for me. Please hurry, I've been up all night traveling." She gave him back the phone.

"At least he'll know you're in town. If you have an address, I'll give you a ride."

Her eyes grew wide, and she swallowed visibly. The thought of a ride in a stranger's car in a strange city at six in the morning was terrifying. The young man acted as if he hadn't seen a thing.

"My name's Benny, what's yours?"

"Please leave me alone. I have enough to deal with right now."

"Listen, there's an open coffee shop right over there." He pointed catty-cornered across the street. "No sense waiting outside on your feet, especially since you don't know how long it'll be before your ride shows up."

She was hungry and the thought of a plate of bacon and eggs was nearly irresistible. But if she headed for the coffee shop, she knew he'd tag along. If she even mentioned breakfast, she knew he would buy. The stress of the past twenty-four hours had finally broken her down, and her lower lip began to tremble. Oh, how she wanted to go to sleep and wake up in Colton's arms. But her knight in shining armor was a street-wise, low life with a scraggly mustache who she knew was up to no good. She turned and walked back into the terminal.

She went to the vending machine and bought a tiny bag of peanuts for a dollar. When she had eaten, she fell asleep in a plastic seat, and it wasn't until shortly before eight that she woke up. Her nightmare was still in the building, standing in a corner, talking to another societal reject.

There was no one she knew in Dallas except Colton. There was his family, his mother and sisters, who lived in Garland. Exactly, where was Garland? She hadn't gotten their phone numbers. Why hadn't she? The girls were quite friendly.

Marie looked around and saw nothing but faces. No one to talk to. No one who appeared to have the slightest bit of extra mental capacity to help a young girl. She was going to have to find a shelter. Being downtown, places like the Salvation Army should be nearby. She sucked up a deep breath. For an instant her body tingled with the euphoria of freedom though she knew she'd stepped into a fresh pile of horse shit in the process. Escape from the farm had been her all-consuming goal, and she hadn't thought about what may lie ahead. She had to get away from the bus station--she had to find a shelter. With some quick directions to the closest one, she headed out the door, up the street.

CHAPTER TWENTY-THREE

Melissa reluctantly took Morgan to the 'sleeze barn' to work that night. She would pick her up, too. With her help, Morgan was not long for the topless stripping business, but first, they needed Colton back in Dallas.

Back home, Melissa went through his mail to see if there was anything he needed to know about right away. There wasn't. It was all bills, solicitations, and coupons.

But the very next day, an envelope arrived that had been forwarded from Colton's place of work. It was from Marie. Melissa tore open the letter and read it. Immediately, she was back on the phone with Colton again. She had talked with him for an hour last night about Morgan. Now she read the letter to him word for word. He had her read it again.

In the weeks since his back fully healed, Colton

had been asking anyone and everyone if they knew what might have happened to Marie Rucker. The helpful woman in the high school office confirmed his suspicion that as long as he had known her, Marie had not been on a school field trip.

He had to get a lawyer due to Rucker's charges, but the lawyer said the matter would likely be dismissed. It was his word against Rucker's and Colton's prints weren't on the conveniently found crowbar left in the front yard. In fact, the police had a growing interest in Rucker. He hadn't filed a missing person report until Colton brought it to their attention, and now Rucker acted like a distraught father that all he wanted was his daughter's safe return.

The letter from Marie, filled Colton with joy, an exuberant hope only the deeply worried can know. He danced in place, and thanked Melissa profusely. Every fiber in his body seemed to take a deep breath. Now he had something to go on. He looked up San Angelo on the map. In the middle of the night, he headed that way.

He took Highway 67, a meandering Texas state road to the southwest. The letter said she was with relatives at a farm. He prayed she would still be there. Secondly, he hoped the adults she was with were reasonable people. Colton could think of no logical reason why she would be there, out of school, and without the ability to communicate. But he would soon find out.

He found the address on the mailbox below the name, Winters. There was a quarter mile drive up a gravel road to an expansive ranch-style home beside a huge metal storage shed, fenced pens and cattle handling equipment off to one side, and a huge barn atop a shallow rise that could easily be seen from the road.

The door was answered by a heavyset woman with a pensive if not downright pitiful expression, and her gaze seemed to look past him as though she had been deep in thought on another topic.

"Good morning. My name is Colton King. I came by to see Marie." Colton was there to neither mince words nor play games. He knew he had the correct address. Either Marie was here or whoever lived here knew where she was. The last word he spoke flipped a switch in the woman's brain and she said, "Just a minute." She went to her phone and called Rob. "There's someone here about Marie."

Rob drove from the barn on a four-wheeler. Bonnie stepped outside, and closed the front door. This conversation would take place on the porch. When Rob approached, Colton extended his hand, and reintroduced himself. Rob didn't reciprocate, but stuck his thumbs in his back pockets. His face became troubled, and his eyes focused squarely on their visitor.

"Marie and I are friends. She's been missed by a lot of her friends back home. I understand she's here?"

Rob's expression turned from impassive to disappointed. "You don't know where she's at?"

It took a moment for the question to hit home, and Colton hoped it wasn't bad news. "No, I don't know where she is, or I wouldn't be here. Has she been   here?"

"Yes," Bonnie admitted, "but she's been gone five days."

"Gone?"

"We tried to keep tabs on her, but she got away," Rob said, in his slow Texas drawl.

The way he said 'got away' like she was some loose heifer that broke through the fence burned Colton's ears, and he could feel his indignation beginning to boil.

"She's been gone from Spinler since, like Christmas. Has she been her all that time?"

Bonnie nodded.

"Why?"

Bonnie adopted a conciliatory attitude and tried to explain. "I don't know if you know, but her mother died late last year. Her father said she was having a hard time adjusting, and a stay out here would likely help her the most."

"And Marie's mother was . . .?"

"My little sister," Rob said.

Colton looked at the two of them and felt like he was talking to children. "You know Marie is of age. Did she consent to this arrangement?"

"Yeah," Rob said, "but she still lives at home, and she's in high school. We wanted to help her father out."

"How would taking her out of her normal routine be helpful? You ever think of that? I mean, really, children lose their parents all the time, and they don't need to go to a psych ward to get over it. She never threatened to slit her wrists, did she?"

Colton looked and saw two forlorn and despondent faces. "Maybe it was you--" and he pointed at Rob. "It was you who needed her around. I've been told she looks just like her mother. Could that be the reason you wanted her around because you couldn't get over losing Margie?"

"Look, young man, we want her back safe and sound. I don't care if it's here or in Spinler or anywhere. We just need to find her."

"Did you call the sheriff? You may not know what clothes she was wearing, but you know what she looks like?

"Yes, we filed a report the day after we found her gone. But we don't know if she got a ride or in what direction she went."

"But she's not here? Colton asked.

They both shook their heads.

"Good, then you won't mind if I take a look in the house?"

"No, young man, you're not going in the house. We told you everything we know, and we want Marie back as bad as you do."

"Listen, old-timer, and listen good. I'll go straight to the authorities about you holding an adult against their will if you don't let me look through the house."

"Get off my land."

"Okay, have it your way you sun-stroked, plow boy, but you might as well get ready to sell this spread--half to the lawyers you're going to need, and the other half to your niece."

"Get off my land or I'll call the police."

Colton laughed in his face. "You two got big, big problems ahead. You can count on that," Colton said as he got back into his truck.

As he headed back to San Angelo, Colton knew Marie was smart enough to know east from west, and the direction the county road ran. She would head east, to either Dallas or Spinler. Of those two towns, Dallas was by far the most likely choice. If she was hitching, the roads to Dallas would have more traffic. Besides, Spinler was farther away. If she had any money at all, she might try the bus station, and he drove into San Angelo to find it.

The information from the man at the ticket counter was discouraging. The bus line did, in fact, ask for an ID from their riders, but any document would do--an old student or military ID, name on a blood donation card or social security card, all easily forged or stolen. The bus line was in the business of selling tickets, not checking to see if someone was legally representing themselves. But the records were kept in the back office, and the manager was out to lunch. Colton waited.

Colton immediately approached the man when he returned to the terminal.

"Sir, I'm looking for a girl who I believe took the bus to Dallas only a few days ago. She's alone and in great danger. I need to know if Dallas was her destination."

"Listen pal, runaways are as common as house flies in summer. I don't have time . . ."

"No sir, she was kidnapped--by her father- and held on a farm outside of town for the last five months. Please help me. I have the dates."

The man groaned, and went to a file cabinet.

"It would have been last Tuesday or Wednesday, the 10th or the 11th. I don't know what part of the day, but I'm sure of the days."

The man let out a deep breath of exasperation, and began flipping through the files. "We had three buses headed for Dallas both days. What is her name?"

"Marie Rucker." Colton knew she had her driver's license, and she was proud of it. If she took the bus, he prayed she'd used it instead of something with another name.

"Well, she didn't leave here on the 10th, at least not using her real name. He searched the next file. And there it was. On the last bus out that day, almost the last name on the passenger list, he saw the name, Marie Rucker. The terminal manager stared at it for a moment, as though the name had suddenly appeared. "I can't believe it. In all the years I've been here, this is only the second time I can remember finding a traveler someone was looking for." He turned to Colton, smiled, and showed him the name. "She took a bus to Dallas on the night of the 11th."

"Thank you. Thank you so much."

"Good luck, son"

CHAPTER TWENTY-FOUR

Colton headed straight for Dallas. Two young women, his girlfriend and his little sister, occupied his thinking, and he was both relieved and incensed. At least he now knew where Marie had been since he last saw her in his hospital room. Increasingly, he feared for her safety. She was still at least a week ahead of him. In the big city in that amount of time, she could be anywhere, with anyone, caught up in anything.

More immediately, his mind harbored vengeance. Melissa's phone conversation detailed Morgan's descent into the adult sex trade, and it was none other than their birth father who had taken her there. She hadn't been forced into prostitution, but Morgan's trusting and sensitive nature would bear emotional scars. Her experience would be no less debilitating in the long run. Their birth father, Heath Diebold, had been warned. After his beatings had killed their biological mother, neither of them wanted anything to do with him.

And yet, he had come around again. With Morgan's innocent, receptive, friendly nature, Heath sucked her into the business without any concern for his own daughter. Without any great leap of logic, Colton knew he did it to make a buck. The man was a selfish manipulator, void of any morals. Colton would free his sister of his threats and bondage.

Back at their house, the girls greeted him with loving hugs that seemed to drain the fear and sadness from them. They were quick to ask him how his burns were healing, and he told them they were much better. He asked about Brenda, and was told she remained lethargic, semi-conscious, and deeply depressed. Her mind had shut down. Maybe her medications kept her mental decline from worsening, but there were no signs of her improving. Colton sat beside her bed, held her hand, and talked to her. If she heard or comprehended anything, no one knew. But Colton wanted her to know he was at home. He would continue to touch and talk to her as often as he could.

He hadn't been back at the house an hour when he sat Morgan down, and told her of his plan for the night.

"I know where he lives," he told the girls. "You're not going to work tonight or any other night," he addressed Morgan. "We'll go over to 'daddy's place' before six. You go to his door and offer him $200, because you want out. When I come to the door, leave immediately, and go back to the truck."

This day had finally come. Somehow Colton

knew it would ultimately come to this. For the first eight years of his life. he heard nothing at home but the constant screaming between his parents. His mother's only failure was having sex with Heith Diebold, and getting pregnant. Heath's disregard and abuse of Donna always stemmed from him being forced to marry her, although he'd likely fare far worse on the female open market.

But the total revulsion Colton had for his birth father ran far beyond being subjected to his tirades. The man's repeated beatings finally killed his mother, and now, he'd pulled his daughter into the adult sex trade. There was no magic curtain with which to cloak his lies. Her own father was grooming her to be a call girl.

"Okay, you ready?" Colton said.

"I'm ready."

Colton was pumped. He had never been more ready to deal with a festering sore than tonight. "Remember, when I come to the door, go straight back to the truck, and don't touch anything."

Morgan walked onto the old motel property, and located unit #6. She knocked on the door, and good old dad answered.

"Hey, sweetie, getting ready for tonight?"

She nodded. "I can't do this anymore. I brought you $200 to square up."

A smile grew on his face, and he laughed. "Oh sweetie, you're just tired. It's just swaying to the music, and showing some skin. There ain't another job nowhere that pays such good money for doing next to nothing."

"Do you want the money or not?"

"Get your ass over to the shop, and put on a frilly outfit. You like that pink, see-through one best, don't you?" He laughed again. "Then, make sure your tight ass is back down here by six tomorrow or I'll come looking for you with a switch." Heath laughed some more. This time a raucous belly laugh as though he'd said something clever.

Colton stepped in the doorway, and Morgan slipped away.

Heath was still amused at himself, in a welcoming and agreeable mood. "If it ain't my boy. Look son, I'm making money for the family." There was a pause. Heath had yet to register any concern over Colton's appearance. "Where's Morgan? Tell her to come back."

Colton stepped into the unit and caught Heath with a powerful, unsuspected uppercut that put the middle-aged man to sleep with one crunching punch. If Colton hadn't broken his jaw it would be a miracle, because his fist caught him right on the chin. Heath crumbled like a rag doll. Colton shut the door with the heel of his boot.

Colton took a ¼" rope from his pocket, twisted it into a garrote around the man's neck. He lifted Heath's head and chest, slung him over his back, and strangled the man with his own dead weight. Colton held him up until his back ached. Even then, when he was sure the man was dead, he held him up by the rope for another five minutes. When he let him down, Heath's face was a dusky color. His lips were outlined in blue. Colton listened for a heartbeat. There was none. Colton wanted to stab him or shoot him to be sure, but he couldn't. No blood, no noise. He certainly looked dead, and Colton knew, if the man survived the amount of time Colton had him dangling, he would have to be visited by an angel.

Colton rolled up the rope and put it back in his pocket. He was neither elated, sorry, nor sad. After so many years of physical and emotional abuse to those around him, Heath Diebold had to pay. His biological relationship to the man had lost any meaning years ago. Strangling a dog hit by a car, howling with the excruciating agony of a broken back, would have saddened Colton more than what he had just done. If what he'd done wasn't justice, Colton still saw it as fitting. Some people just don't deserve to live.

Colton turned off Heath's phone, and put it in his pocket. Then he used a wash rag to open and close the front door, and he walked back to his truck.

Morgan didn't know what had gone on between Colton and Heath, and she didn't ask. It would never be discussed, their birth father's name never mentioned again. The couple who ran the porn shop didn't know Morgan's phone number or address. She was again a free woman.

And while Colton garnered an ephemeral satisfaction from what he'd done, the act gave him no pleasure. He had killed a man, his birth father. It was the greatest transgression of civilized and natural law, and yet, he was simply thankful it had gone as cleanly as it had. Would he do it again? The thought jumped quickly through his mind, and he dismissed it immediately, for he had no intentions of the sort. He only did what he did because he had to. But there was plenty of evil in the world. There were many men who deserved a similar demise. The contemplation was more distressing than the act itself, and he forced the subject from his mind.

He was devoted to his sisters, his mother, too. He would do anything to help and protect Morgan, Melissa, and Brenda. But now, his thoughts turned to his dearest love, Marie. He stepped into the truck, gazed upon Morgan's beautiful face, and a wave of heartsickness engulfed him. If only he could have rescued both young women tonight.

When Heath missed two consecutive days of work without calling his employer, his parole officer was notified. No one answered the door at Unit #6. The parole officer used his master key to open the door, and was met by a swarm of flies. Heath's black body was decomposing nicely in the dank, warm temperature of the unit.

The police were called, but when the detective in charge found out the deceased was an ex-con the matter was quickly relegated to the back burner. It could have been a robbery or a revenge killing--the possibilities were almost endless with a victim of Heath's background. The other tenants of the old motel were interviewed, but no leads materialized, no one around the place was considered a suspect. Heath's employer said he kept to himself while at work. The case went cold.

Though Morgan quit showing up to dance, the

Cook's who owned the porn shop had no way to contact her, and went about their business. The cops didn't know about the porn shop connection, and the Cook's didn't know Heath was dead. According to the paperwork at the parole office, Heath Diebold had no next-of-kin. So the good taxpayers of Dallas County gave Heath a brand new pine box, and he was buried in an unmarked grave in a city-owned plot. Even the grave diggers didn't spend as much as ten seconds saying a word or two over his grave once they had finished filling in the hole.

CHAPTER TWENTY-FIVE

M arie found the doors to HARVEST HARBOR. The woman at the counter was friendly, but all business. No one could come in until 7 pm, but she could register now for a cot since she was a first-timer. Marie was as hungry as she was tired, so she went to a store full of magazines, trinkets, drinks, and packaged sandwiches. She bought food and walked to a nearby park.

Benny watched her leave the bus station, and knew her most likely destination. He called ahead to one of his cohorts, actually his boss, a guy named Jason, who patrolled the five-block area where three shelters were located. Jason got her description, easily located her, and watched her walk to the park.

Jason shaved every day, part of the job description. He wore clean dress clothes, and his hair was trimmed. His smile could be captivating, He projected a sincere interest as an attentive listener. Humor or sympathy came from him easily as the moment required. His ace was his smooth diction and choice of words. With any suspicions of his target dissuaded, his bait an expression of true empathy, Jason sunk his hook. With his bright eyes and pleasing appearance, few ever got away.

He entered the park opposite from where Marie sat, and took a bench without ever looking her way. He played with his cell phone until she finished her food, and he stood and walked her way.

"Good morning," he said as he stopped well in front of her.

"Hi."

"Haven't I seen you somewhere before?"

Marie looked at him, and pursed her lips. She hadn't been exposed to the polished, yet obvious, comeons of young men. But it didn't take a lot of experience to know to avoid a snake. She didn't know for sure about this guy, but she had been hours without seeing a bed and had become increasingly defensive. That he was well-dressed meant nothing at the moment. The sheer fact that she was alone had her antenna on high alert, but the reception was fading. She had the will, but not the physical stamina to continue to fight.

She didn't respond to him while she stuffed her food packaging in a plastic bag.

"That doesn't look like much of a breakfast."

Again, Marie said nothing in hopes her silence would send him away.

"My name is Jason. I'm married, okay?" He extended his ring finger. "I have a little girl. I work in that building right there in the computer department on the night shift. I'm headed home, but

I could take you to a real restaurant."

Marie listened quietly. She didn't know if she was listening to a tall tale or a genuine offer to help. She was becoming too tired to think straight. She knew no one. She would get nowhere in this town by herself. The man looked professional, his words sounded sincere. Even the most astute person would be challenged to see through his con. Marie wasn't stupid, but she was exhausted and hungry.

"I would appreciate that," she said.

Jason nodded in a relaxed manner as if his offer of assistance was the least he could do. She followed him for two blocks to his car, a shiny red Chevy. He worked his way out of downtown, and headed east on Ross Avenue. He pulled into a well-known neighborhood diner, and turned to her. "Let's go in" he said, "and get you a real breakfast. I think I'll have a cup of coffee." Marie ordered bacon and eggs with a tall glass of milk and ate it all as though she hadn't had a thing to eat for a week.

"So did you just arrive in town or have you been here a while?"

"Just this morning," she said.

"Someone's supposed to pick you up, right?"

"I've got a phone number, but no one answered. I've got an address near Forest and Webb Chapel Road. You know where that is?"

Jason nodded.

"I know some friends in Garland, but I don't know their exact address. If I could see a Garland phone book, maybe I could find it."

Jason quit stirring his coffee, and gave her a very sweet and engaging smile. "Now, I might be able to help you there. I live in East Dallas, that's toward Garland. If you'd like to come by and meet the wife, I'm sure we can locate your friends, and they can come and pick you up."

Marie returned a forlorn, frightened, hopeful expression, a look Jason had seen many times before. It was the look of a desperate teenage runaway. There was a place in Jason's hardened heart for adolescents in such a situation. For Jason was not a pervert, a sadist, or a pedophile. He was a businessman. The girls would teach Marie the ropes, and Benny and his crew would manage the street. Jason paid for breakfast, and escorted Marie back to the car.

CHAPTER TWENTY-SIX

M elissa had more things to do at home than anything school could match. Her father was in prison, her mother was in a deep state of depression. Her sister had just been rescued from the clutches of the sex trade, and her brother was searching far and wide for his girlfriend who had escaped the confines of ill-advised relatives only to become lost in the urban wilderness of Dallas, Texas. A moment of peace came when she carved out time for herself, and wrote to her father.

The letter writing was therapeutic. The fabricated tales gave balance to her chaotic life. Shouldn't there be more joy in life? Why must there be suffering, especially among the innocent? She sat beside her mother's bed, and when she finished writing, often read them to her as she slept.

Dear Daddy,

I hope and pray you're doing well. I do hope you're able to keep busy. It's been almost six months since you left, and that's good, in a way. Time can fly by when you stay busy. Mom talks about you every day. She has come to the conclusion that your crime was the result of the stress of your job. Though the acts were misguided, the purpose was well-intended. Mom said that very thing herself. She misses you a lot. She has forgiven you for everything.

Morgan has gotten engaged. It's the same guy I wrote about before. His name is Byron, and he's from Athens, Texas. They make a great couple. You'll like him. Morgan told me they weren't even contemplating marriage until they graduate.They want to wait until you're out so you can be in attendance.

I don't know what all Colton is up to, but he's always in a good mood, and he comes by the house at least twice a week. As for me, I have finals coming up. My schoolwork is all A's, except math which is a B. I'm very happy with that. Besides, math has never been my best subject. Please take care of yourself, and keep busy. I know you'll be home soon.

I love you, daddy Melissa

Colton went to the Dallas bus station and hung around. He bought a soda, and stood in the corner. He grabbed a section of the newspaper, and sat down to read. No one approached him or asked him any questions. He checked the bus departure and arrival schedule numerous times to make it look like he was there for a reason. Most importantly, he watched every bus that arrived.

The ridership of every bus was as similar as a row of crows sitting on a telephone wire. There was the heavy-set Hispanic woman with large paper bags with handles, filled to the rim, and two children in tow. Two old women on an excursion together, and the half dozen migrant workers. Colton watched the sleepy travelers disembark, and he kept watching specifically for those one or two individual souls.

Late in the morning, a bus arrived from Houston. She was the next to the last one off the bus. Her blonde hair was tucked up under a ball cap. She carried nothing with her. She wore a jean jacket over a dark blouse, blue jeans with rips at the knees, and tennis shoes. Most noticeably, she kept her eyes down. Colton could see how that was an immediate tell. If she had been expecting someone to meet her, she wouldn't be looking at the floor.

She bought a candy bar from the vending machine, and stepped outside. If she had a phone she had yet to use it. Almost immediately, she was approached by a young man with a mustache made of peach fuzz more than real whiskers. Colton could see them both, and the young man had an easy smile. She wasn't taking offense at whatever he was saying, but his body language reminded Colton of a snake, the way he dipped and shuffled, and ever so slightly, invaded her space.

Colton's stakeout of the place appeared to be

paying off. One thing was certain, the two didn't know each other before meeting, The girl hadn't moved, but neither was she talking. If anything she was caught in the spell of his double talk, and she didn't know what to say. She didn't look a day over fifteen. All girls of that age have an innate beauty borne of youth. She could have been the homeliest girl in her high school class, but she maintained the undivided attention of the hustler.

Then Colton saw her head jerk, her eyes widened with apprehension. Something he said crossed a line or raised a question she was not inclined to explore. Colton made his move. He walked from the terminal.

"There you are, dear. Sorry I was late. The car is around the corner." He took her arm, and they began to walk. "I'm an undercover cop to get you someplace safe," Colton quickly whispered.

"Hold on, stud, we're talking." He poked Colton in the back.

"We appreciate the Dallas welcoming committee. Thanks." He and the girl kept moving.

"Don't get smart with me, I was talking to the young lady, so butt out."

Ignoring his comments, and with their backs turned away, Colton whispered to her again, "Do you think he has your best interest at heart?"

"No,"she said, and began walking faster.

"Okay, asshole, but you better not come down here again."

As they turned the corner, Colton looked back and got a good look at the kid with all the smart mouth retorts. "All talk. He's just a punk. I'll get you somewhere so you can clean up, and regroup. Would you like that?"

"Yes, yes. Thank you."

Colton drove to the house. He spoke in generalities until they got there. With Melissa and Morgan around, they would find out all about her. The girls didn't seem all that surprised when Colton walked into the house with a strange girl. They smiled at each other, but waited for Colton to explain.

"These are my sisters, Melissa and Morgan. I found her at the bus station already being hit on by a street punk. I could tell he was up to no good. I just wanted to get her out of there. I thought I'd wait until we were all together for her to tell us whatever she wants us to know."

"Can I get something to drink?"

"Sure," Melissa said, and she went to the fridge for a Pepsi.

"I left Houston last night to get away from my abusive stepfather. I don't know anyone here. I just bought the ticket that would take me the farthest." She took off her ball cap, and a thick mane of golden hair fell across her shoulders. Her eyes were a brilliant bluish-green. She had a pensive, reserved look, much like Morgan's somber expression, and Colton could already tell, she could say more with her eyes than mere words could ever convey.

"How old are you?" Morgan asked.

"Fifteen."

"And your name?"

"I'm Marie."

Colton couldn't believe his ears. Never in a

million years. For the moment he shook it off even as he saw Melissa and Morgan on the edge of laughter. "Well, I'm Colton and I'm not a cop. When I saw you, it looked like you were getting in a bad way, so I stepped in."

"I'm so thankful. You're my guardian angel."

Her words hit his brain like a stroke, and he literally felt woozy. The coincidence of her name and endearment was disconcerting on one hand, but then, rather funny. Melissa and Morgan watched him closely, both wide-eyed and smiling, as he regained his composure.

"I'm almost fifteen myself," Melissa said. You can stay here for now, for sure. Maybe we can find something to do together this summer. Come in the kitchen. I'll get you something to eat."

Colton pulled Morgan into the bedroom. "I think I may have something to go on. A creep was on her within minutes of her arrival. That's probably what happened to Marie, but I don't know exactly who might have taken her or where. I'm more scared now for Marie than before I went down there." He sat beside his mother and took her hand as he continued talking to Morgan.

"Keep your eyes on this girl. I think she's a legit runaway who needs help, but just make sure she doesn't try to scam us."

Morgan nodded.

Colton leaned over, and kissed Brenda's cheek. "You look lovely today, mom. Have a wonderful day." And he kissed her cheek again.

Jason pulled into a driveway of a nice looking home with a two-car garage and brick veneer siding. Marie felt at ease in his presence. He assured her that finding the address she was looking for would be no problem. But when they entered the house, her adolescent brain went on point. A person doesn't need to be taught to avoid spiders and barking dogs. She felt her heartbeat pound against her chest, and a hollow feeling invaded her guts. She took a deep breath in an attempt to slow everything down.

There was no way the woman Jason introduced her to was his wife. His mother, maybe. Her hair was in curlers, and she wore a house dress in the middle of the day. But her face was made up like she was about to go on stage, and she'd smoked two cigarettes before Marie hardly had time to sit down. There was no mention of a child in the house.

"Tell Jeri and me your story, Marie," Jason said as he took a seat beside her on the couch. Jeri went to the kitchen, rattled ice into her glass, and made herself a drink."

"Why?" Marie asked. "Are we going to be neighbors?"

Jason smiled. He liked a bit of spunk and backbone in the girls. His inclination to beat girl's buttocks black and blue was legendary among the regulars, but Jason was not cross--not yet. Besides, he would never hit Marie in the face. She was way too pretty for that. "Just curious, that's all. You arrive in town all alone with no one to pick you up." He shrugged his shoulders.

Marie stood, her breathing decidedly faster. "You

said you'd help me. People ARE expecting me, but we got our times mixed up. That's why I don't have a full address. I didn't think I'd need it."

Jason listened patiently, and ignored every word she said. "Would you like something to drink?"

"No, I want to see a Garland phone book. Come on, mister. I'm just a kid. I thought you were a super nice guy. I can't do what I know . . . Dear God, you might as well hold me for ransom. I'm worth $100,000."

Jason let out a genuine laugh. "Jeri, you hear that? She wants us to become kidnappers, send out ransom letters, and all that."

"Get a bundle all at once," Jeri said, more interested in adding more liquor to the drink.

"Yeah, except kidnapping is a federal crime."

"Well that's what you're doing, aren't you?" Marie was emphatic. "If you don't let me walk out that door, you're guilty of kidnapping."

"Sweet thing, you think too much. Nobody is kidnapping you. You've just had a change in employment plans, and decided to stay with us for a while."

Marie put her hands to her face, and curled up into a ball against the far armrest of the couch. "Jeri, show this young lady the accommodations," Jason said.

"Hey, girlie," Jeri yelled as he stood in front of her. When Marie dropped her hands, Jeri threw off the wig with the fake curlers, and threw open the robe. It was a man behind all the makeup.

"This is our resident transvestite," Jason laughed, as Jerry pulled Marie into the back room and raped her.

CHAPTER TWENTY-SEVEN

By August, eight months after Daniel set foot in prison, Brenda lay in her bed, and stared at the ceiling. She had been in bed with debilitating depression for most of that time. Her pillowcase was crusty from dried tears and slobber. Her nightgown was soiled even though both were changed regularly. A person can't sleep for twenty-four hours a day, so at this moment, when lucid thoughts fought to scrape back the sadness in her soul, Brenda revisited the landmarks of her married life.

She met Daniel at the pizza shop, a tall, handsome Dallas police officer who took her to a movie. It was the happiest day of her life. She knew from the beginning he had his eyes on her. She knew now, he was only settling. Her parents and all of her sisters were present at her wedding. Within a year she and Daniel had bought a house and welcomed Melissa into the family.

Two years after that, they adopted Colton and Morgan. That was another high point in her family history. Children were a blessing no matter their sex, age or where they came from.

Daniel became her rock. They made decisions together, laughed together and cried together. Now he was gone, yanked without warning from her life. Daniel's sudden death would not have been any more painful because he was gone just the same. The ability to visit him once a month for twenty minutes was hardly a consolation, so she never made the trip to the prison. For three to five years she would have to struggle on her own. Such prospects were debilitating, and if he did ever come back, nothing would ever be the same.

But the depth of her despair was magnified by the sight of Marie. She looked just like her mother-- the woman whose memory had squeezed all happiness from her husband—for he had lost her on one summer day twenty years ago, and had never gotten over it. Should Colton ask for Marie's hand in marriage, it would be more than Brenda could stand. Marie would be around Daniel, now her father-in-law, on a fairly regular basis. Daniel would never forget Marie's mother, Margie. With Marie around as a constant reminder of his lost love, Daniel would never embrace Brenda as the true love of his life.

Melissa came in the room with a chicken salad sandwich, and a glass of milk. She saw her mother awake. "Feeling better, mother?"

Brenda closed her eyes, and shook her head. "Just leave it, dear. But I would take a hug."

Melissa reached down, and hugged her mother. "My sweet, baby girl. Thank you for helping me." Brenda kissed her cheek.

Brenda reached for her antidepressant pills, a prescription that served some patients equally well as a sleeping pill. Brenda poured a handful of the pills into her palm, and swallowed them with milk. She closed her eyes, and rolled over in bed.

When she woke up, she was gagging, and in pain. Her pillow was wet with spittle, and her throat aflame with heartburn. She forced herself to sit up. She drank the rest of the milk. Her head was woozy, and she fell beside the bed as she tried to stand. Still, she had to make it to the TUMS in the bathroom. Her esophagus felt like it had been pulled apart. She could never rest with the discomfort she was experiencing.

She crawled to the bathroom. There, she took a handful of antacids, and a couple of pain pills. Then, as she stood, and struggled to maintain her balance, Brenda grabbed another bottle of equally powerful antidepressant capsules, and downed the whole bottle of thirty pills. When she turned back to her bed, Brenda fell in the doorway where Melissa found her. Her body, cold and chalky white. Brenda Kline King was dead. She died of a broken heart long before she ingested the pills.

CHAPTER TWENTY-EIGHT

The three King children had dealt with a steady string of life's collisions. With their father incarcerated, Morgan pulled into the sewer of nude dancing, and Colton's Marie missing without any clues as to her whereabouts, they had stood against the gale of misfortune with their mother's staunch resolve as their rock. But she had fallen into a deep in depression, sleeping twenty hours a day. The girls had cared for her day and night. They had played the songs she was known to love at her bedside. The doctor gave her a prescription for an inhaler that shot medicine straight to her brain. They even gave her bubble baths, and when she stood to rinse off, they would turn the faucet to cold, and spray her down with hopes it would shake her from her doldrums. She screamed at the cold water spray, but once dried and dressed, she never made a comment about it.

Now she was gone, overdosed. Whether it was accidental or on purpose really didn't seem to matter. They were all knocked to their knees, blindsided by a blow that almost makes it impossible to remember your own name. Colton knew the girls would take what was to come, funeral and all, worse than him. He was already numb with sadness, at a loss of what to do next, but he would shake it off. He had to. But the day Brenda died, he felt like a little boy, alone in a snow-covered forest, with a bear tracking him and getting closer.

Daniel had left him the keys to his file cabinet. If there was a life insurance policy on his mother, he had to find it. Two of Brenda's sisters came to Dallas. They took Morgan and Melissa with them to the funeral home to make arrangements. Colton felt the weight of debilitating sadness. This was the woman who had taken him under her wing when he was but eleven, and nursed his heart and soul back to a playful, rambunctious kid no longer afraid of adults and the world around him.

But he was losing time tracking Marie. Every passing day put her farther away from him, and in greater danger. As far as he knew, she had been in Dallas less than a day. At this point, she may not even be in Texas. The unknowing, the uncertainty provided fertile soil for dreadful scenarios, and Colton was restless and sad, constantly racking his brain on what to do to find her.

Runaway Marie from Houston went with Morgan and Melissa throughout this period of a family's mourning. It was as though there had been a passing of one of her own. She stuck with the girls, especially Melissa, and comforted them.

Colton finally became aware of all he must now do. Besides burying his mother, he had to get back to work. His parents still had a significant savings account, but the money to make the mortgage payments, and support the girls, would not be there unless someone was working.

Most importantly, he had to find his Marie. Gnawing ignorance, without the slightest clue of where to pick up her trail, was more painful than his mother's death. At the funeral, he didn't hear a word the preacher said as he held Morgan and Melissa's hands, and when it was time to pass by the casket, he only glanced at his mother's peaceful face, and moved on.

Another eight days were lost in the search for Marie from the time Brenda died to the day she was buried. Finally, Colton came up with a plan. He called his father's old patrol partner, Officer Garrison to ask about missing persons, and how such cases were handled by the department. Garrison's words were not encouraging. Unless there was a solid lead to work, most missing person files were left open, but not worked. Runaways were common, means of transportation ubiquitous, and many abductions were the minor's parents using children as pawns in marital squabbles.

Even though Garrison hadn't heard from Colton since Daniel went to prison, Garrison liked the young man. He liked the whole family, and was deeply disappointed when Daniel got himself caught up in criminal charges. Garrison always had his suspicions that Daniel was getting into fights outside of police work, but he chose to ignore the signs. He felt sorry for the family when Daniel was sent away, and if Colton had a legitimate law enforcement concern, Garrison would do all he could to help.

Colton told Garrison about Marie's father, being taken to the farm against her will, and her bus ride to Dallas. He told him about what he saw in his hours at the bus depot, and that he felt sure Marie had fallen into the clutches of sex traffickers. Garrison agreed, Colton was probably right.

"I've got a desk job now, "he informed Colton, "but I work closely with two detectives. If you have something solid to follow up on, let me know."

Colton immediately brought up his personal rescue of Marie from Houston. "The people who work at the terminal can't do anything about it because these perverts work in rotating shifts, and the ticket sellers don't know who is who. But I'll bet you a hundred bucks, whenever there's an arrival, scum bags are waiting to see who gets off the bus."

"I guarantee you there are many girls, and no doubt some boys," Colton continued, "who are being held for the sex trade, who are praying for someone to save them. Some of them may have run away for a good reason, other maybe just as a lark. But if we can rescue them, there would be a lot fewer missing person cases, and a lot more kids thankful to be back home."

"I agree with you one-hundred percent, Colton,"

Officer Garrison said.

"We need to put a wire on a lure, listen to their conversation, find out where they go. And I have the perfect girl for the job."

"You never cease to amaze me, Colton. When you have an idea, you are ready to put everything behind it. Well, good news. I work with a Detective Lawrence who would gladly put in some hours on a task like this, especially if you and I do the tracking and monitoring. There are a few things to consider. We can learn a lot if your girl wears a wire, but most wires are monitored from a set location. If we try to follow her all over town, it's easy to lose the signal. But if you're game, it's worth a try. I can get the van and a technician to help. I'll call you in a day or two when everything is set up, and you can bring in your girl."

With a backup in place, Colton gathered the three girls, and laid out his plan. He would take one of the girls to Fort Worth to take the bus for an early arrival in Dallas. He would be waiting, dressed differently than before, and see who latched on to her with sweet talk and promises. Melissa demanded to be chosen, but first Colton wanted to address another issue.

"The new school year is about here, Marie, but I can't get you into school without a transcript. If I request one, your people back home will know where you're at. So you'll have to read Melissa's books and have her go over what's she's studying."

"I can do that."

"Yes, yes. We can study together," Melissa was intensely excited.

Colton smiled. "Okay, and one other thing, Marie. You need to change your name. What's your middle name?"

"Christine."

"Okay, Christine it is, and our last name is King. We have to stick with that, girls, if we want to protect her for the time being. She's a cousin."

"Is that okay with you, Christine?"

"That's fine. That sounds like a perfect idea." And Colton saw the happiness on her face, especially in the thankful expression in her eyes.

CHAPTER TWENTY-NINE

J eri, the transvestite, handled Marie like she was an old pro at getting screwed, and he chuckled as he held her down, and pulled off her clothes. Marie screamed and fought back, but it was useless. In that hour, her virginity was stolen, and her spirit died. When he was through with her, Jeri left her on the bed to sulk and cry. He had busted a wild bronc. Now she would become an obedient, gentle ride, a woman who made money for the crew without complaint.

As she lay on the bed, clutching a pillow, Marie's heart was beyond tears. Her body had been handled like a piece of meat, and her love for life crushed under the boot of depravity. She wanted to die. No one would ever love her now.

She hurt physically as she lay there, and for the moment, defeated. But she was not ashamed because she had not been shameful. Her drift toward self-pity quickly faded when common sense told her the only thing that mattered was survival.

She knew little about sex, but they would teach all the disgusting things she needed to do to get men's money. If she could live with herself, she would fight for another day. With time, Colton would find her.

Morgan was chosen for the mission. She was older and had already experienced the slick lies of professional perverts, and would be better able to handle herself. She was fitted with a wire at police headquarters, then Colton drove her to Fort Worth and got her a ticket. The bus would leave at 7:50. She would arrive in Dallas around 8:40 after the thirty-mile trip. Colton would be waiting.

He wore cowboy boots, tight jeans, a western shirt, a fake mustache and a dusty, broken-down cowboy hat. Nothing better than hiding in plain sight. People who glanced his way quickly went back to whatever they were doing. But Colton had other worries far more disturbing. Besides the wire, Morgan carried a signal device that sent out a ping every two seconds. When he bought it, Colton thought it the perfect electronic device to backup the police wire, and keep Morgan safe. Now, he wasn't so sure. He would try to follow her, but she could get out of range of both electronic devices. He still might lose her. Even if the pinging indicated her vehicle had stopped, he would have a hard time telling exactly what building she was in unless they were actually close enough to see her vehicle. The odds were against him. Besides, if knocked on doors were even answered, the person or persons who held her could hardly be expected to tell him the truth.

It was too late to cut and run now. The combination of the transponder, and the wire gave Colton a measure of assurance. This was his little sister, after all. He'd give his life for her. If anyone should harm her, they would pay. One man already had, their birth father. Colton had made him pay the ultimate price for his immoral and greedy transgression. In spite of his apprehensions, the this mission had to go forward.

Morgan stepped cautiously from the bus, and looked the part perfectly, like she'd been on the road for weeks. Her hair was gathered in a ponytail, and wrapped in a bun. She wore no makeup with baggy pants and ripped tennis shoes. She looked like she'd come from central casting, a lost and alone vagabond. She bought a soft drink, and wandered through the terminal, taking a few quick looks at the arrival and departure signs. Then she stepped outside.

She had barely leaned against the building when a young man approached, and whispered in her ear. Morgan moved away, went back inside, and headed to the bathroom. Colton bummed a cigarette, and played with it as he stood against the wall. The guy pestering Morgan wasn't the punk he saw harassing Christine. Colton didn't see him anywhere, but Colton didn't need someone to draw him a picture of how the game was played. There were probably dozens of pimps in sheep's clothing ready to buy a tired and frightened young girl a meal, and offer them a place to spend the night.

When Morgan returned from the bathroom and went outside, another young man stepped to her side. He was ruggedly handsome with black hair and an easy smile. Colton could see it all from his vantage point. The guy wore a dark blue polo shirt and blue jeans with several days of whiskers. Morgan played her part right along. Be aloof and disinterested in the beginning, then get more and more receptive. The guy was experienced with his double talk and probably thought he was prince charming reincarnate. But when he got an inkling of a smile from gorgeous Morgan, his ego likely got a thrill as good as sex.

"I'm broke," Morgan confessed. "I spent my last dime to get here from Lubbock. I'm trying to get to my aunt's house in Richardson."

"That's up north. I'm headed that way. I could give you a ride."

"It wouldn't be too much of a bother?"

"Not at all. It would be my pleasure."

Colton saw the two of them getting friendly. He exited another door, bought a paper from a newsstand, and leaned against the building while he listened to them. When they headed to the parking lots, Colton was thirty paces behind. They got into a silver Lexus. Colton got the tag number before he sprinted to the communication van in the next lot over. The Lexus headed north on Highway--75. Colton and the police listened in on a bunch of generalities about what he did for work, and why she came to Dallas. They both had their fabricated stories well in mind.

"I need to stop at the house on our way, and let my wife know I got Gary on the bus, and it left on time."

"Can't you call her?"

The guy smiled at Morgan. "Won't take a minute. We're almost there."

The communications van was right on their tail. The signal from both devices remained strong. And then, the most horrible thought crossed Colton's mind. Up to now, his only concern had been could they maintain contact. But now he realized--once inside a dwelling, would she be forced to take her clothes off? What if they raped her within minutes of her entering a house? They would find the wire. They would know she was a plant. Colton told Garrison to get closer to the Lexus. His sister's pretty face, if not her life, was in danger.

The Lexus pulled down an alley near old downtown Richardson. There was a string of parking spots under a hail-damaged tin carport behind an overgrown apartment complex. The place looked unused, and Colton saw the back doors and windows of several units boarded up.

"Come on in. We'll just be a minute."

"Go ahead," Morgan said, "I'll wait here.

"Suit yourself. Would you like a water?"

"Yes. That would be very nice."

The police communications van parked at the end of the alley. The technician explained that with a signal as strong as the one they were receiving, and the fact that it was no longer moving, meant they were within steps of the girl. Garrison called for backup, then he and Colton made their way cautiously down the alley.

The man came back from the house, a bottle of water in his hand, and a woman by his side. The woman looked dreadful. She appeared to have slept on her face, if she'd gotten any recent sleep at all, and her age was anyone's guess. The guy popped a button on his car remote so all the doors unlocked. He opened Morgan's door. "Get out."

Morgan acted shocked. The knowledge, the prayer, that rescuers were nearby didn't stop the dump of adrenaline that exploded throughout her body. Morgan got out of the car, but acted miffed. "You said you'd take me to my aunt's. Why the hold-up?"

"Shut up and do what you're told." The guy's tone had changed completely.

The woman took hold of her arm fairly gently. "Come this way."

Colton and Garrison saw it all, especially the back door they entered. Colton walked behind one more unit and to the front, got the exact address, and returned to Garrison.

"Backup will be here any moment," Garrison said. "Two officers will approach the front. We'll go in the back."

"We need to hurry. If they find that wire on Morgan she may be in real danger."

In the van, the technician listened to a conversation about her aunt. The abductor wanted Morgan to call her, tell her she made it safely to town, and that she was going to stop by some friend's house for a few days. The guy doubted her story. She was a runaway like all the others, but it was best to be sure. He didn't want a missing person report filed on this girl.

Knocks came at the front door. The woman ran to the backdoor to make sure it was shut and locked. Knocks came again. "Police, open up."

"Dammit! They followed us." He turned to Morgan, "or you set us up." He grabbed her arm and slapped her so hard she hit the floor.

"Help," she screamed.

A battering ram hit the front door, and kicks could be heard breaking in the back. A bull horn was at the window now. "Everyone inside, come out with your hands up. Do exactly what I say unless you want to get shot."

The old front door was a weak bulwark against the battering ram, and within seconds the police breached the barrier. "On the floor, hands behind your head." The guy and the woman were quickly put in cuffs.

As they searched the apartment, one room was locked without any visible way to unlock it. But the people inside had already heard the word 'police' and were pounding and screaming for help. The police kicked in the door. The sight that greeted them was hard to believe. Five young women were living in a room built for maybe two. Two slept on a bunk bed, the rest slept on the floor. They all looked shell shocked and lost. The smell was horrible like a bucket of used diapers had been set in the corner. Of the five, one of them looked like a regular. She might have been there because they fed her, who knew? She would be taken to the women's shelter. If several days later, she wanted to be back on the street, that was her business.

But the other four were in tears. They hugged the police, and couldn't quit crying. Detective Lawrence would be in charge of all of them, to find out where they came from, how long they had been in Dallas, and where was home. Colton hugged Morgan, and gently brushed her cheek. It was red, but the slap hadn't left a mark. They watched as each of the girls came from the bedroom. Colton felt the pride of accomplishment and a happiness for rescuing four young women from another day of bondage and degradation. At the same time, another feeling overwhelmed him, a sadness, a deep and unyielding despair, for none of the girls were Marie.

CHAPTER THIRTY

Nine months in the big house and Daniel had gotten used to the routine boredom. He was not in segregation, but rather, a building of non-violent, white collar criminals. Even though Daniel crimes were violent, he was an ex-cop, and there was no place else to put him where his life wouldn't be in constant danger. The inmates in this unit lived in a huge bay, slept on bunk beds, and listened to each other's complaints, laughs, farts, and the incessant clanging of metal lockers.

There were times when Daniel wished he had his own private, plexiglass enclosed cell. But really, he didn't. Being able to move about was a blessing. In fact, many areas of the cell block from the mess hall to the activity yard were marked, not by fences or barbed wire, but by a two inch yellow line on the concrete. Step over the line without permission, and get reduced privileges, and six months added to your sentence. It was a simple directive, yet a bitter pill to swallow. Grown men ordered not to step on a yellow line.

Entertainment to pass the time consisted of watching TV, reading a book, playing gin rummy, or conversation. Some of the biggest crooks with the longest sentences also had the biggest egos. Somehow to them, stealing a few million dollars from elderly people who had trusted them was a feather in their cap. They bragged on and on about how they'd duped their clients without the slightest hint of irony or remorse. They would be using a walker before they ever saw the outside world again, and they'd never get to spend another penny of their ill-gotten gains, because most stolen funds not already been spent were usually recovered and returned to the victims.

Daniel was thankful for Melissa's letters. He received an average of two a month, and he read each one at least a dozen times. He hadn't heard from the others, especially Brenda, but Melissa kept him abreast. He felt bad for himself, but even worse for them--leaving them high and dry. Melissa's positive news gave him the assurances he had hoped for. His family had tackled the bad situation with spirit and determination. When he returned, whenever that may be, Daniel would throw himself into making restitution to them all.

Colton and Morgan rode back to the bus station in the van with Officer Garrison and the police technician. Not much was said during the ride, but the quiet glow of a job well done was more satisfying than a rowdy round of high fives, if not more so.

Back in Colton's truck, Morgan lay her head on his shoulder. "I'm exhausted," she said.

"I know you went through a lot. Are you okay?"

"I'll be fine, but there were a few times I got worried. I mean, the guy was calm and collected, pleasant and friendly, and all the while, I knew he was as deadly as a water moccasin."

"Was there ever a time you thought he might actually be taking you to your aunt?"

"Not really. He was in too much of a hurry to drop everything else a person might be doing. It never felt right." She looked up at her brother, and hugged his arm. "I never could have done it without you close by."

"We were close," he said. "You were never out of contact with both the transponder and the wire."

"I don't want to do it again, Colton, at least not right away." She gazed at him with an expression that revealed all he needed to know of the stress she had endured. He would not subject her to a similar ordeal--not soon anyway, not at all if he didn't have to. "The cops have to be with us," she said. "It's bad enough to be the bait for these creeps. I have to know there's lots of backup."

Colton gave her a sympathetic smile. "You did great. Now just relax. Don't tell Melissa or Christine too much, or they'll think it's exciting."

"I don't think Christine has any such illusions, but I don't think I'll tell them much of anything."

Colton knew how Morgan felt. Besides hoping for a successful sting, he had been worried for

Morgan through the entire ordeal. But he was just as concerned about Marie. If she had fallen into the trap of being a streetwalker, then she had already been violated. That alone made him sad, but he didn't love her any less. He would scour Dallas for her until his dying breath. If she had been taken elsewhere she might be lost, but he would never stop looking.

Colton went back to work full-time. After work, he would get something to eat and go to the bus station. The buzz in the terminal was much greater in the evenings than the mornings, and no one gave him a second look. When a weary and unattached young traveler exited a bus, they had few choices. As darkness descended, the sewer dwellers found their way to the bus station. Colton found himself spending more time saving lost children than he spent searching for Marie.

CHAPTER THIRTY-ONE

One night, Colton ran into a lad at the bus station candy machine. He looked to be twelve. Colton wondered how he'd ever been sold a ticket. Come to find out, he was sixteen. His name was Danny. He had left a small town not far from Salina, Kansas, and had taken the bus south on I-35 to Big D. At first, when Colton said a word to him, the cords in the boy's neck stood out, and he returned a penetrating stare. The boy's antenna was up, receiving signals from all directions.

"You've been in here a while. Where's your ride?"

"What the hell. What do you care? Why don't you worry about yourself?"

"Suit yourself, but see those two guys over there? They're into boys. Boys about your age, I would say. And more of them come around after seven." Colton let the words sink in. The huge clock on the wall read 6:30. "So if you end up sleeping in the station all night, keep your hand on your belt buckle, and don't go in the bathroom."

The kid swallowed hard, and searched Colton's face for the veracity of his words. "Good luck," Colton said, and he went to a seat across the room. Ten minutes later, the kid came and sat beside him.

"Listen, mister. I have relatives in Carrollton. You know where that is?"

"Yes."

"I have relatives, two boy cousins my age, but they don't know I came to Dallas. I just wanted to get away from my little town in Kansas before school starts. I know I have to go back. I have the address. . . I don't suppose. . .?

"Are you sure?"

He shrugged his shoulders. "I know I'm kinda stuck, and you seem like a good guy."

"Okay, well I'm Colton, and you are?"

"I'm Danny."

"Let's head out and see if we can get you up there before your relatives go to bed. Because, let me assure you, you don't want to spend all night in this terminal."

"Thanks, mister . . . Colton."

Colton knew one night away from his relatives would not ruin the boy's schedule. It might turn out to be the most fun of his entire trip. He drove to the house, and honked the horn. "Come in, Danny. I have a surprise for you." Melissa was the first to the door. "Get the other girls. We have a guest."

Christine was quickly at the door, too, and the girls watched in confused delight as Colton brought a male visitor into the house. Morgan came out from her bedroom.

"Danny, these are my sisters. They are excellent cooks, and they always love to fix something for company."

"Not so fast, Colton." Morgan stepped forward, and took Danny's hand. "Hi, I'm Morgan." The other girls introduced themselves.

"I'm Danny. I'm from Kansas." He had never seen three such attractive young women in his life. His astonished expression got the younger girls laughing.

"You can stay here tonight, in your own bed, in your own room. I'll look on the map for your relative's address, and I'll take you there on my way to work in the morning. That sound okay to you?"

"That sounds great."

"We can call your relatives tonight, so they know you're in town. Be sure and call your folks first thing when you get over there."

"I will. I will."

Melissa and Christine scrambled through the kitchen to prepare a meal. No one had had a real supper yet, so the timing was perfect. Christine made a salad while Melissa prepared sloppy joes.

"So you traveled all the way down here from Kansas by yourself?" Christine asked.

Danny nodded.

"I tried the same thing from Houston. I found the trip's not a problem. It's what do you do once you arrive. Colton rescued me. You may not know it, Danny, but if there was no one around to pick you up, then Colton rescued you, too." For a while, everyone ate in silence.

The younger girls wanted to know everything about Danny. It wasn't that they hadn't seen boys as cute, but this one was in their home. He was good looking, farm rugged with a tan face and rough hands. Danny was flattered. Both of the younger girls seemed slightly smitten, for if Cupid had missed with his arrows, they both had still been hit with glancing blows.

After dinner, Colton showed Danny his room. "Here's your bed for tonight. I'll sleep on the couch. The bathroom is right down the hall. Let's call your relatives." Danny's uncle answered the phone. He was surprised, but receptive. They would expect Danny tomorrow.

"Thank you, Colton."

The girls cleared off the dinner table, and set out a board game. Morgan played with them for a while. She had gotten a second grade teaching job at an elementary in North Garland, and had to report tomorrow for teacher training. Finally, Colton needed to go to bed, so he moved the game to the girl's room, where the three of them played well into the night.

It was seven in the morning when Colton had to leave for work. Not only was Danny up, but both the girls. As the youngsters said goodbye, Christine gave Danny a slip of paper. "That's my address," and as if on cue, Danny gave Christine a kiss on the cheek.

"I'll write," he said.

Melissa beamed. She wasn't jealous or even thought like that. Non-judgmental, full of love and fun, Melissa. She was simply happy when anything even remotely positive took place.

Colton smiled to himself as they readied to leave. A chance meeting may turn into a lifelong relationship. That's the mystery, the randomness, the unpredictability of life. How foregone conclusions sometimes never materialize, and long shots of tremendous odds slide together in a perfect fit. He was glad he had brought Danny to the house. He wished him the best. He wanted the best for his three lovely, intelligent, beautiful girls, too. But most of all, he wanted one more.

CHAPTER THIRTY-TWO

Marie's life descended into an unimaginable fog of degradation. On the street, her usual attire was heels, nylon stockings, hot pants and a tube top that showed her midriff and shoulders. She carried a handbag over her shoulder with little in it--maybe some chap stick, and a bottle of water. It had a hard-to-see interior compartment where money could be safely kept.

Jason and his entourage of streetwalkers moved from the Jupiter Road area after an incident had cops constantly watching the motel they used. Jason picked a location of late night dance halls and fancy restaurants, plenty of foot traffic, and middle-aged men with money and a hankering for female companionship. Jason made a deal with the owner of an older motel named The Skyline to have the exclusive use of five rooms at the back of the building.

The men Marie had to entertain were a mix of

middle-aged losers who still looked pathetic in a three-piece suit. Few of them were actually single, and all of them had money. They were looking for something new and fresh. They weren't forking out a hundred dollars to have sex with a forty-plus-year-old woman who reminded them of what they had at home.

Some of them had no patience for pleasantries. They wanted quick sex and be gone. Marie swore they must have jackrabbit DNA in their blood. They all wanted her to take her clothes off, but not all were after sex. Some just wanted to tell their troubles to a beautiful stranger. Marie gladly engaged in thirty minutes of chit-chat to avoid being laid upon. But there were the disgusting ones, where she had to disassociate her mind from her body to keep from screaming. Lecherous, tobacco breath, sweaty pigs who wanted to touch every inch of her body, and talk about erotic pleasures as though they had invented sex.

Jeri, the transvestite, was in charge of the large loft, the top story of an old warehouse they used as sleeping quarters. The girls were primarily fed burgers and soft drinks. Jason did two things for the girls, both in his best interest. Each new girl got a a doctor's appointment so they could get birth control pills. Second, was the motel. He wanted the girls to stay safe, and he didn't want them running away.

NEVER GET IN A CAR. TELL THEM TO MEET YOU AT YOUR ROOM.

The weeks dragged by. Marie lost track of time. There were never any clocks or calendars around. The girls were not allowed to have phones. From the middle of the afternoon until midnight, most days, Marie Rucker let strange men use her body up to eight, nine, or ten times a day. At $100 a pop for regular sex, Marie never saw a dime. She would not consent to kinky or aberrant sex, and if any john pushed the conversation in that direction, she told them it would be $500. So far, she never had to.

Neither Colton nor Marie knew that she was less than twenty miles from the house. The months passed, and winter came. But her Colton never did. The light of her soul left her beautiful blue eyes, and the tone and suppleness of her skin began to suffer. The girls had one bathroom to share, a huge porcelain tub with claw legs, a rusted-out sink that constantly dripped, and several mirrors hung on the walls. Jason bought them toothpaste and tooth brushes, cheap skin cream, sanitary pads, hair brushes, and all the fake jewelry they cared to wear. That was it.

Marie no longer cried. Her tears and prayers had brought no one to her rescue. Even though she learned the general routine between her and the johns, every encounter was a new experience, and wearisome. Some of the 'customers' giggled as though they were ten years old, and had found a pair of girl's panties. The morose dudes were probably sullen because they didn't have two brain cells that worked together at the same time. Still, she never knew, even in the relative safety of the motel room, that she hadn't landed a serial killer who just wanted to get her alone. If you're being smothered, you can't scream. If you're dead, you can't tell one of the pimps outside to come to your rescue.

She kept plugging ahead. Life was better if you kept Jason happy. She had already seen his flexible leather paddle, about six inches long and four inches wide with a thick, wooden handle. It looked like a beaver tail, and she had watched as Jason used it on Amber. Ten swats on her butt and the backs of her thighs. Her skin was black and blue for weeks. Keep pushing and praying, Marie thought. This was not going to be her only life. Someday something would change.

CHAPTER THIRTY-THREE

Initially, Colton thought he could get a lead on Marie at the bus terminal. She arrived in Dallas at the station, and that was where the punk mouthed off to him when he rescued Christine. He reckoned if he ever saw the guy again, he'd get a lead on the whereabouts of other enslaved girls. But the demand for sexual services was far beyond what the bus station could supply. The depot was just another flowing river where people came and went, never to return. Hookers came from anywhere and everywhere; some with pimps, some without. They popped up like ants drawn to a candy bar whenever and wherever demand called for their services.

Colton knew Harry Hines Blvd. was flush with long-legged girls in skimpy outfits, and too much rouge. But he decided to concentrate his search for Marie in an area of east Dallas not far from Fair Park. Among the old prairie-style houses and antiquated apartment buildings was an assortment of porn shops, liquor stores, massage parlors, and pawn shops.

Colton slowly drove the side streets. Girls were often on street corners, slightly hidden in the bend of drooping branches. They wanted to be seen by potential customers, but avoid the roving eyes of the police. After a conversation at the truck window, Colton was told where to meet up. Pimps often blocked the way, wanting payment before he could enter the room, but Colton was having none of that. He didn't know if the guy might take off with the money or if the woman was actually inside. He would pay the girl, he told them. If that wasn't to their liking, Colton walked away.

He quickly realized, he wasn't interested in paying a hundred dollars for a girl to take off her clothes just so he could ask a few questions about who she worked with. Thereafter, he cruised the streets with plenty of twenty dollar bills, and a picture of Marie. Every girl who would talk to him, and look at the picture, he'd slip a twenty, whether they had any useful information or not. He moved around the area from Garland Road to Skillman, from Munger to Ross. For three months, he worked a full day at his job, and another six hours every night looking for Marie. Then, one evening, a girl's eyes lit up when she saw the picture. She didn't know the girl's name. She couldn't even recall where she had supposedly seen her, but she was adamant that she had. As Colton gave her a twenty, their eyes fully met.

She was a slender girl with short-cropped auburn hair curled under around her neck. A spate of freckles spread across the bridge of her nose under dimly lit hazel eyes. She wore a windbreaker in the evening chill, and tight, green spandex athletic pants that ran down to the knee. "What's your name," he asked.

"Tiff . . . I mean Tammy. Do you want a date, too?"

Colton hesitated before he spoke. All the while he maintained eye contact with the girl. "Not tonight. I'm just looking for this girl. Her name is Marie."

And as Colton watched, the girl's eyes became wet, and he saw a desperate pleading overtake her expression. "Will you help me too?"

She spoke each word with great effort. The plea was heartbreaking. Colton swallowed and felt the sadness in her request, but he moved immediately, instinctively. He would save her if he could. "Get in the back, right now. The door's unlocked." As the girl scrambled into the back seat, Colton quickly moved out-of-sight, and made numerous turns as he drove from the neighborhood.

Colton was fully aware that the girl's pimp undoubtedly saw her jump into his truck. The description of his vehicle along with the license plate number wouldn't have been that hard to note. He knew, that in order to rescue the girl, he had to get as far away from East Dallas as possible. The search for Marie would have to wait. But he didn't head toward the family home in Garland. He needed to spend some time with this girl--alone. If she could remember anything about Marie, he had to bring it out of her.

Colton stuck to the side streets as he worked his

way north. He pulled into an old motel right on Highway 75, and parked at the back of the lot. "Stay here," he told her. "I'm going to get a room, but I don't want anything from you. Just to talk. Okay?" She nodded. "I'll be right back."

In the light of the motel room, Tammy looked underfed. Her hair appeared clean, cut and styled, and her nails were bright red, professionally done. But her eyes projected fear, manifest by any one of the million terrors that can rise from the deep recesses in the human mind.

"Take a big breath, Tammy. No one is going to find you, and I will help you. You can stay in this room tonight after I leave, and tomorrow at ten, I'll have a police officer come to pick you up. So, please relax. You're going to be safe. Your life is going to change."

"Thank you. Thank you, mister. I was so afraid I'd jumped into the wrong truck. You can't trust no one on the street. . . but I trust you."

"My name is Colton. How old are you, Tammy?"

"Eighteen."

"Where are you from?"

"Shreveport. My parents kicked me out when I started smoking weed and staying out late."

"Would they take you back if you quit doing those things?"

She reluctantly shook her head. "They don't have much money, and I'm eighteen now. They made my brother move out when he turned eighteen."

Colton didn't like the sound of that. A teenager with no home, no job, and no place to go. The police would take her to the women's shelter. The people there would try to find her a job. They would let her stay there as long as they could. There was also a good chance she'd run into an old associate which would complicate her efforts to escape the lifestyle. Tammy would be a hard case to help in any meaningful way.

Let me ask you again about the girl in the picture I showed you. You said you saw her at one time. Tell me where."

Tammy rubbed her forehead and temple as she sat in a chair. She did appear to relax a bit. Colton leaned froward from his seat on the edge of the bed, and waited intently for any meaningful words from the girl's mouth.

"I've been in Dallas, I'd say eight months. My pimp had me and this other girl working the west side of White Rock Lake in the area where Gaston Avenue meets Garland Road. It's a white, upper-class neighborhood, but there's plenty of dance halls, liquor stores, restaurants, and a pool hall in the area." Tammy sighed deeply, then raised her head and looked directly at Colton. There were another bunch of girls working the same area, so we moved closer to town. But that's where I saw your girl. I'm sure of it. We passed each other several times on the street, but never said a word to each other. But I haven't seen her in months, so I know it was back by the lake where I saw her."

Colton wrote vigorously. Her words gave him a new, refreshing, and greatly needed infusion of hope. "Can I get you something to eat?" he asked.

Oh, could you get me some chicken," she said,

her voice imploring him as though she had never tasted it. "Chicken sandwich, chicken fingers, I don't care. And some fries and some milk."

Colton began to smile. "Yes, I can handle that. Stay right here. I'll be back in twenty minutes." As he went for takeout, Colton knew he could call Garrison in the morning, and get a police car to the motel. Not that the police department was in the business of playing taxi, but Garrison would do it for him even if he had to make the trip himself. Officer Garrison was his friend, and fully behind his efforts to locate Marie, and rescue vulnerable teenagers. As for Tammy's long term prospects, Colton didn't know. He couldn't take her home. He already had four mouths to feed including his own. She didn't even have a high school diploma, kicked out of her home, no skills, no money to her name, and she'd been a prostitute. Even Christine hadn't been through all that depravity. But what would she find at the women's shelter. The question gnawed in his gut. He had to quit worrying about every poor soul he ever met. He brought her the food which she devoured.

"Wash up and get a good night's sleep, Tammy. Thank you for everything you told me. I really appreciate it. A car will be here in the morning to take you some place safe."

Tammy's eyes began to well up with tears, and she tried to smile. Her voice couldn't speak, but Colton saw the thankfulness in her expression, and he closed the door behind him as he left.

CHAPTER THIRTY-FOUR

The weather turned cool, and all the girls wore sweaters or windbreakers, but the heels, black embroidered see-through stockings, and hot pants remained. Marie saw the Christmas lights, the giant candy canes, and wreaths that decorated many houses and stores. She knew it had been a year since she'd been kidnapped, and taken to the farm. Half of that time she'd been a victim of human trafficking. She wondered if she'd ever be able to have children of her own.

The typical clientele were middle-aged men who couldn't get it at home or didn't want what was there. Some wanted to role play distinctive scenarios to fulfill particular fantasies. Playing mommy was the most disgusting. Not only did the johns put their lips to her breasts, but they became nauseating, immature two year olds when they did.

Lower Gaston Avenue was a thriving area of bars with live music and nice restaurants. Across the street was a 2000-seat concert theater, and a gentleman's club. Traffic rushed from the city on Garland Road, and the junction of the two avenues on the southwest side of White Rock Lake was an entertainment district unto itself. The area pulsated with humanity ready to party well into the night. Along with the diners and music lovers, there were plenty of men who cruised the side streets in the area looking for young female flesh. The next day, Colton spent the entire afternoon and evening walking past all the businesses along Gaston. The buildings were two-story. They rose up in front of a cliff that faced the lake less than a hundred yards away, and the bright glow from the businesses reflected off the water.

As the evening pushed past 9 pm, and darkness gave a stark back-drop to the numerous lights of the area, Colton saw a scantily clad girl stepping in and out of the light beside a concrete retaining wall. Colton's instincts took hold. He sprinted in the girl's direction, and hollered the name 'Marie.' But the girl turned and ran, up the few steps to the landing above, then into the blackness behind the building. By the time Colton was atop the steps, she was gone.

He had been so close, but he had better things to do than lament one missed opportunity. He knew the girls used different names on the street, but if that girl had been Marie, she would have stopped. He knew she heard him. He was on the right track; he could feel it. Maybe he needed help, another person to assist him in finding the girls. He thoughts turned to Officer Garrison. Garrison was pushing forty-years-of-age, same age as Daniel. He would fit the part of middle-aged man looking for a good time. He could also maintain his composure, keep his calm. Although he had never met Marie, after all the pictures Colton had shown him, he knew Marie's face like he knew his middle name.

Garrison was all in when Colton spoke of his plan. "So you think you've narrowed down where she's at?"

"Almost certain," Colton said.

"Okay then, I'm with you, but I'll have to change my schedule." Detective Lawrence, who was the lead detective in the missing persons department was fully behind the plan, and with some coaxing, the Captain approved the change in Garrison's work schedule. For the next week, he was officially on duty from 4 pm to midnight.

The two men went to the area at 7 pm. They each went in separate directions to find young women looking to be their 'date.' Colton found a woman at the back of a parking lot, hardly a place to be well seen. As he approached, Colton saw the dirt area behind the parking lot that was accessible from the residential street in back. From the looks of the packed earth in one parking spot, numerous cars had come there to seek her out.

She had copper red hair down to her shoulders. Her breasts appeared non-existent and she needed dental work. Colton quickly determined she was pushing forty really hard, if she hadn't already crossed the barrier, and if she ever saw fifty, it would likely be a miracle. He tried to show her his picture of Marie, but the woman gave him a snide look like he was a bill collector, so Colton walked away.

The first woman Garrison saw stood beside the side door of a honky tonk. She had a gorgeous mane of thick, black hair that fell across each side of her face as she turned her head. Her bangs were too long, fluttering in front of her eyes. She wore a pink sweater without a bra, it appeared, with hot pants and black see-through stockings even in the briskly cool evening.

"Hell-o, mister. Would you like a date?"

"I think I would. How much?"

The girl hesitated. "You're not a cop, are you?"

"No, no, you don't need to know what I do, but I'm not a cop."

"I didn't ask you what you do. Maybe you're hard of hearing?" Garrison could tell she was bored, disinterested beyond comprehension. Her motivation to deal with him at all likely rested on the opportunity to get out of the cold. She was all business. There was no glint of fun in her eyes or even the tiniest flicker of a smile from her lips.

It was Marie. Of that, he was sure. His police training almost overtook his behavior, and he wanted to take her, hold her, and tell her everything was all right. He wanted to tell her that Colton was just down the street. But he didn't. The men had a plan. So he waited.

But the excitement in his mannerisms alerted the girl. She studied his face more closely, his clean shaven face, and trimmed business haircut. "Regular's one-hundred dollars. You got that?

Garrison nodded.

"I'll be in Room #20 in that motel back there."

She pointed. "Be there in ten minutes."

Seated in a silver Lexus in a parking lot beside the lake, Delroy, a tall Jamaican with a complexion of glistening dark chocolate watched the exchange between Garrison and Marie across the street. It was his job to watch Marie and three other girls as they sauntered along Gaston Avenue, and when one of the girls lined up a 'trick' to phone Benny back at the motel.

Garrison and Marie's conversation seemed normal in the beginning. But then, Marie became agitated. Her body language changed. Whatever the reason for her change in attitude, Delroy became wary. The crew liked sexual transactions that were uneventful. An unwanted possibility was always at the back of Delroy's mind. Anyone could be a cop. Anyone could be a kidnapper. Anyone could be a serial killer.

With a rendezvous apparently set, Marie disappeared between two buildings. Delroy was about to call Benny when the man who had spoken to Marie yelled down the street, and began running up the block. Delroy turned in his seat, and saw the man beckon to another man on the other side of the road. The two men met up, spoke to each other for all of ten seconds, and the second man sprinted to the corner, and disappeared up Garland Road, headed to the motel. The man who had talked to Marie remained on the sidewalk for a few moments, then entered the pool hall.

Delroy couldn't get his phone to put through his call fast enough.

"Don't let Marie go to her room," he told Benny. "Something fishy's going on. Another man is headed for the motel than the man she talked to."

"Any idea who it is?"

"Hell, I don't know. Just keep her out of sight. In fact, better keep her under wraps the rest of the night. I'll bet money those two men were looking for her in particular, and they'll keep looking for her even if she doesn't show in her room."

"Whatever you say," Benny replied. "I think I see her coming now."

Garrison moved out to Gaston Avenue as quickly as he could without creating suspicion. Colton was a block away about to cross the street toward the gentleman's club. Garrison broke into an all-out sprint. "Colton, STOP! Come back."

Together on the sidewalk, Garrison inhaled deeply to catch his breath, and then said, "I found her."

Colton grabbed him by both arms. "Are you sure?"

"Very sure, Colton. There's an old motel along Garland Road within walking distance. She'll be in Room #20."

Colton ran to the corner, then headed for a lit sign several hundred yards up Garland Road. The concrete drive into the motel had more tar in the numerous cracks than concrete. The trees in the area had surrounded and smothered the old structure, and as was typical with businesses like this, a sign in the office window prominently read-- Hourly and Weekly Rentals Available.

Colton's pace slowed as he reached the front of the motel, and he walked along the building in the direction of rising room numbers. As he moved to the back of the motel, he passed a man sitting in a metal chair smoking a cigarette. His ballcap was pulled down over his eyes, and he appeared to be half asleep. Colton gave him a glance and moved on. He had lost track of time, but he felt sure more than fifteen minutes had passed since Garrison had spoken to her. He stood in front of the door to Room #20. He took a deep breath, and put his hand on the doorknob. His body had dumped a flood of hormones into his bloodstream, and he didn't know how he felt--excited--thankful--ready to hold his precious Marie again.

He turned the knob and opened the door. The room was little more than a closet, musty and dark. He flipped the light switch. He walked to the tiny bathroom, then he looked back behind him. No one was there. Quickly, he shut the door and sat on the edge of the bed. Maybe she hadn't arrived yet. But two seconds later he was up. He paced the room. He could wait no longer knowing Marie was nearby. Maybe she simply changed her mind. Maybe her pimp told her to go to another room. The possibilities were endless. Colton was frantic.

He left the room, and approached the man smoking a cigarette. "Excuse me. Did you see a young women go into the last room down there?" He pointed.

The man pushed back the cap on his head and Colton saw--it was the punk from the bus station with the scraggly mustache. "I seen several come and go," the young man said.

Colton grabbed him by the jacket with two hands, and yanked him from his seat. Colton kneed him in the groin, then smashed his head into the building with this right shoulder. The fellow fell in a heap, and Colton clocked him with a doubled-up fist across the side of his head.

Colton checked the guy's waistband and jacket pockets, and retrieved a pistol from his coat as his victim groaned, and rolled around in a fetal ball. Colton had no idea how many girls worked with these perverts, and he didn't know how many there were of them. But if anyone thought they were going to stop him now, they better bring a small army, because Colton was ready to shoot some SOB in the head if it meant finding his Marie. All the commotion brought a middle-aged man, still hoisting up his pants out of the room closest to Colton. The girl with him glanced outside, then slammed the door, and locked it from the inside. The girl wasn't Marie.

He wished he had told Garrison to stay with Marie if he ever found her. What a stupid idea to want to surprise her in a motel room. That was probably the last place she'd want to be found. She would cry and be thankful--her prayers finally answered. But why? Why did he think showing up in a motel room as a prospective john was the way to go about it? He felt sick, the idea was so stupid. He gathered himself. At least he knew she was nearby. When he found her, he would rush her out of the area, and take her someplace safe. And he would find her tonight.

Colton was about to grab the man on the ground, pull him to his feet, and make him talk when he was hit in the back of the head with a small wooden fungo bat. He dropped to the ground unconscious. Two men pulled him to the back of the building and soaked him under an outside faucet. He was left to freeze in the forty-degree evening. They took the gun from Colton's pocket, and helped their friend to a nearby car, then rounded up all of their girls, and left the area for the night.

When Colton came to, twenty minutes later, he was freezing with a lump on his head the size of a golf ball. He made his way back to Gaston Avenue, and found Garrison. Garrison immediately saw Colton's injury, and got him to his car. Medical attention for his head was the first order of business, and the whereabouts of Marie drifted on the cool evening breeze. Now she could be anywhere.

Back at the warehouse, Jason was livid that his crew felt the need to cut the evening short. The early departure mean at least a thousand or two in lost revenue, and someone had to take the blame. Jason pulled Marie in front of all the others.

"Someone was coming to your room who knew you. Who was it?"

"I don't know. I don't know anyone around here." Her eyes glared with confusion and fear. She shrugged her shoulders. "I don't know anything. Really."

"You lying, slut." He pushed her against the wall and made her bend over.

"No, Jason. Don't hurt me. I've done nothing wrong."

Delroy and Jeri forced her torso down so that her butt stuck out, and Jason retrieved his infamous leather paddle. Jason lashed her with ten whacks on the buttocks and upper thighs while the other girls watched in terror. Marie screamed and twisted about, but Delroy held her up. When he finished, Marie dropped in a heap on the floor, and she rolled about in cries of agony.

When Marie quit crying and rolling about, Jason pulled her up, and threw her on a bed.

Don't you ever play games with me, little girl. I say, you've got a personal friend that's looking for you. Well, you can be sure, if he comes around the lake again asking for a date, we'll be ready for him."

Jason bent over Marie and looked closely at her face. "What's the matter with your mouth?" He looked closer. "What's with your lip? Turn it up."

A white lesion ran along the inside of her mouth.

"Does that hurt when you push on it?" Jason 's words were demanding, and he stared at her mouth.

Through tears and strands of hair, Marie pushed on her lip, then shook her head.

Jason turned. "Shit," he said to Jeri. "She's got the clap." He walked with the transvestite to the corner of the room.

Jason ran both hands through his hair, and let out a big sigh. "Now she's double trouble. I'm going to send her up north to Quinn. I owe him a favor, and she'll be out of our hair.

"I can take her to the doc. She can't be sick that long," Jeri said.

Jason looked up and made direct eye contact with Jeri. "I said to send to Oklahoma City. I don't want to deal with her anymore."

CHAPTER THIRTY-FIVE

Two days after he ran into Tammy, Colton went to the women's shelter to find her. She was on a bunk, sitting up straight, looking intently around.

"Good morning, Tammy."

"Oh, hi." She took a closer look, and smiled. It was sweet. White teeth in a pleasant, easy smile. "I'm so glad you came down."

"Why's that?"

"I don't know. Just cause you're here."

"So, how is it?"

"I'm okay, mister. What's your name again?"

"Colton."

She stood beside him, a few inches shorter. Her soft hair rubbed his chin. "Can you take me somewhere, like to eat?"

"Maybe, but let's go outside and talk."

They took a seat on a metal bench in the court-yard. "Who is your pimp, Tammy?"

"A guy named Darnell. He's about thirty. Known

me since I got in town."

"Is he violent."

"Humf." She let out a sarcastic snort, and thought for a moment. "Not really. Just your by-the-book ass hole, in my opinion."

"Will he come looking for you?"

Depends. If business is slow or he has too many girls to handle--he wouldn't."

"So, what do you think about that?"

"I don't want to stay here."

"Okay, let's go tell the desk you're going to out for a while. We'll get something to eat. Do you like chicken?"

She smiled, a wider, happier smile. "You remembered." She tried to take hold of his arm.

"Tammy, Tammy." He was caught a bit off guard, and while he did mention chicken to make her smile, he wasn't ready to be clung to. She lay her cheek against his upper arm, and he felt the pressure of her fingers, and the warmth of her nearness. After his initial surprise at her action, within seconds, he didn't want her to let go. They both lost track of time as they stood in the courtyard. Tammy remained content to touch his arm with her cheek on his upper arm, and Colton remained still, until finally, he reached down and took her hand, then held it with both of his. "Let's go get something to eat, okay?"

By the time they finished lunch, Colton had decided to be responsible for Tammy's safety. He wasn't exactly sure why. She was several years younger than both Morgan and Marie. With the red lipstick, and gaudy mascara washed away, she looked like a typical school girl. Part of him felt as though he'd become little more than a babysitter with the outlay of a lot of time and expense ahead of him to get her back into the normal world. But another part of him dismissed such obstacles. She was too fragile to cast to the wind. Tammy was not beautiful like Morgan or charmingly pretty like Melissa. But she was attractive in her own way. Her skin was about as white as skin can get, and she was taller than the average girl. He had already seen how she could throw her puppy-eyed expression his way, and it reminded him of Melissa. He could not leave her. For now, he would take her home.

"Do you have anything still at the shelter?" he asked.

"No. All I have is the clothes on my back."

"Okay, I need to take you back to the shelter so I can get to work. But, I'll be back at five. Wait for me."

He dropped her off in front of the shelter, and he saw the wetness in her eyes. She folded her hands under her chin, and watched him pull away from the curb, and her gaze followed him until his truck disappeared from sight.

A little after five, Colton drove to the front of the shelter. Tammy was seated on an outdoor bench, anxiously awaiting his arrival. She got in the truck, and fastened her seat belt. "Good to see you again-- Colton."

"I said I'd be here."

"And, I knew you would be." She gazed at him with her puppy dog expression full of both thankfulness and questions.

"Don't look my way with your head down, Tammy. You have nothing to be ashamed about. I'm not ashamed of you. So put you head back, and look people in the eye. We're going to get through this together."

She sat back, wiped her eye, and released a deep sigh. She didn't ask where they were going, and Colton didn't say. A long, rush hour trip to Garland, and Colton pulled up in front of the house. With as many runaways as Colton had brought home, he knew the girls would be receptive. Yet, he also knew they would sense something was different. But they were polite, respectful, smart girls. If he didn't come right out and answer any questions they had, they would ask him about them in private.

Colton rang the doorbell as they entered which had the girls scampering from their rooms. "This is Tammy," he said, as he put his arm across her shoulder. "She's from Louisiana." And he introduced the girls. "Morgan, do you have anything, you could spare, that would fit her?

"I'm sure I can find something," Morgan said.

"We were about to start fixing supper. Would you like to eat with us?" Melissa's question was as if right on cue, and Tammy graciously accepted. The girls fixed pulled-pork sandwiches along with a tossed salad.

All three of the girls surveyed Tammy without gawking. She definitely needed some meat on her bones. But the light behind her green eyes had reigniteed, and her whole face seemed to glow. If she wasn't so hungry, Tammy might have laid on a bed, and simply cried herself to sleep, she was so happy.

Ever since Brenda died, the master bedroom remained vacant. Colton and Tammy retired to the room shortly after supper. "Here's where we sleep," Colton said without elaboration. He went in the dressing area, changed into running shorts, and a T-shirt, then turned on the TV to a football game.

Tammy still stood beside the king size bed with the handful of clothes Morgan had given her. "Is that what you're going to wear to bed?" Colton asked.

Half bewildered, Tammy went to the bathroom area. She hung up a few clothes, then slipped into a nightgown, and put on a robe.

Back in the bedroom, she stood on her side of the bed, but moved no further.'You can get under the blankets if you like," Colton coaxed.

As much as she trusted Colton, she was at a loss as to what was going on. She pulled back the bedspread, and got under the blankets, and lay flat on her back staring at the ceiling. It was too early to go to sleep. Maybe he was saving her a lengthy cross-examination by his sisters. They had already asked her plenty. She was smart enough to figure there was more going on than what met the eye, and she felt pretty sure it wasn't about sex.

Colton hadn't ask her about sex when he first met her, and he didn't bring up sex when he had her in his truck. The only currency she had to repay his kindness was her body. But the way Colton treated her up to now, her instincts told her was one thing he wasn't after. Maybe this was a test. Maybe he wanted to see if she'd revert to her tactics on the street. She would not betray his kindness with a crass overture of sex. She sat up in the bed, and adjusted the pillow behind her. "Whose playing?" When the game was over, they each rolled to their side of the bed, and wished each other 'good night.' But as Tammy tucked the blanket under her chin, she smiled to herself. I wonder if he wants to kiss me?

CHAPTER THIRTY-SIX

Within two weeks, Morgan got Tammy a job at a preschool. One of the employment requirements was a high school diploma, but Morgan knew the owner, and the requirement was waived. Tammy was able to ride to work with Morgan in the mornings, but had to walk the twenty blocks back to the house each afternoon. She basked in the energy, and innocents of the small children. The environment was a balm to her damaged soul, and she looked forward to work each and every morning.

Colton was never home early in the evenings. He continued to search for Marie. He spent another month around the businesses around White Rock Lake, and in all that time, didn't see a single streetwalker, must less, talk to one. Officer Garrison was back to his daytime work schedule, and Colton was left with the gnawing thought that he may have lost his last chance to ever find Marie. They should have carried buzzers or had their phone on vibrate so he could have responded the moment Garrison found Marie. He could have run to where he generally knew Garrison to be. Then within earshot, he could have found him, and the woman with him. Garrison said for sure it was Marie. Why had she not shown up in Room #20 like she told Garrison?He knew it was a question that would never be answered. His stupidity and the loss he felt brought a hollow ache to his chest

Colton was sure that Marie was with a group of woman, all directed by two or three pathetic pimps. Now, he was back to square one. He had no idea where they had been taken or in what area they now worked.

Colton wondered if Marie had ever been arrested in Dallas. Garrison had said her picture had been sent to every police, and sheriff department in Texas, that she was classified as a missing person. Maybe the jails didn't have access to that information. Had she ever been arrested? The question took hold of his thinking, and festered there. He had to step back, and think if there were better ways to search for Marie. But he also had another matter that needed attention, and he decided to tend to it now.

Christine had written her parents. They knew she was alive and well in Dallas. They had no return address to write back, but Christine assured Colton and Morgan that their concern about her situation or whereabouts would be superficial, at best. Her mother was a twenty-four-hour-a-day busy body. She was more concerned about other people's business than the welfare of her own family. Her father, Christine said, was a closet pervert. She didn't want to ever see the man again.

Colton contacted the lawyer in Spinler who had helped him with Robert Rucker's bogus charges. He asked that the lawyer write a letter to the parents stating that their daughter Marie (Christine) wished to remain where she was, and for them to get a copy of her public school transcripts and mail it to his Spinler office. Failure to do so within three weeks, and criminal charges would be filed for sexual battery of a minor. The lawyer called Colton a few days later, and told him the transcripts had arrived in less than a week. The lawyer charged him only $300, and Colton was satisfied. Now he could get Christine enrolled in school.

Days and weeks passed, and the calendar rolled into 2012. Tammy became fast friends with all the girls, but especially Christine and Melissa. She told them without shame of the deprivation, the fear, and the long hours she had to endure. Just talking about her eight month nightmare was therapy for Tammy, and she told the girls, without being graphic, of the terror she faced every time a john laid down his money.

One afternoon, before Colton got home, the girls were at the kitchen table going over Melissa's biology lesson when Melissa changed the subject abruptly, and turned to Tammy. "Does Colton touch you in bed?"

"What?" Tammy smiled. "And give me a good

night kiss?"

"And. . ." Christine chimed in.

Tammy smiled as the younger girls looked at her, their curiosity killing them.

Tammy chuckled as she shook her head. "No, your big brother is a saint. We sleep on totally opposite sides of the bed."

"I would think as long as you've been here he'd at least. . ." Melissa said.

"You have to remember, his heart belongs elsewhere." Tammy interrupted. "He's only helping me like he's helping you, Christine."

"But you're so pretty," Christine said. "You should touch him or kiss him goodnight."

Tammy emphatically shook her head. "I can't do that. He saved me from the streets. If I do something like that, he'll always look at me like a streetwalker. He'll think I'm trying to use sex for my own selfish purpose."

"But you do think he's pretty special?" Melissa said.

Tammy began to cry. "I think he's more than special," she said. "I think he's wonderful."

Melissa and Christine had laughter in their eyes as they tried to console Tammy. "Tammy's got a crush on Colton. Tammy's got a crush on Colton."

CHAPTER THIRTY-SEVEN

Colton began working from morning until dusk. The more air conditioner and furnace repairs he worked, the more money he made. Morgan pitched in with her teaching salary to pay family expenses, but the biggest provider was Colton. Often, he would cruise known locations where prostitutes gathered, but he never found Marie, and he never came up with a systematic plan to search for her. Reason told him she was no longer near. And the streetwalkers that did approach his car, and ask for a date did nothing for him but make him sad. None of them were ever Marie.

Then, in the middle of May, Colton got a call from Garrison. He had been checking the national missing persons database every day since the day Colton told him of Marie's kidnapping. The only pictures shown each day were new missing persons or those that had been found, either dead or alive. "I'm sorry to have to be the one to tell you, pal, but I've come across a picture of Marie, and it says she's deceased. The police is Spinler should be notifying her father, as we speak. She's at the morgue in Oklahoma City. It says she died of an infection."

Colton sat in the grass beside the air conditioning unit he was working on. "Are you sure?"

"I'm sorry, Colton. It's the same long black hair I remember from the night I ran into her. Someone combed it back for a good picture. It's her."

"Okay then. Thanks for calling." Colton's words trailed off in a mumble as he sat numb, and heartbroken. All the work, all the tears. He never had her again after the day she left in his hospital room when she said she'd be gone for the weekend to visit her grandmother. He felt cold as though his blood had quit moving.

When you would do anything to know about someone, often there is nothing more painful than to learn the truth. And when it hurts not to hear about someone, and then, when you do--you wish you had never learned.

He had wanted to love Marie Rucker today, and forever. He remembered how she would look at him with her bright eyes and sweet smile, and her entire expression was full of love. The sadness was overwhelming, but after a few minutes he forced his grief aside. He was too young to wallow in despair. He had a whole life ahead of him. There had been enough unhappiness and regret in his family to last a generation. He would not perpetuate the gloom. He would chart a new course for himself. He would move on. Although he felt sure Marie cried silently for him in her last hour, she would want him to move on. He could only fulfill her loveliness by doing so.

He would tell Morgan and Melissa, but there would be no mourning around the house. He realized all of the worrying he'd put himself through was unhealthy. He would not attend the funeral. He would not waste his life upon her grave. "I'm so sorry, my angel. I'm so sorry."

That evening, after he had spoken to Morgan and Melissa, he took Tammy to the master bedroom and shut the door. In the three months she'd been at the house, working a steady job, and eating regular meals, Tammy had put on weight. Her face was full, and she looked in the glow of health. Colton sat on the edge of the bed as Tammy stood before him.

"The girl I was looking for--in the same situation as you, has passed away."

"Oh, Colton, I'm so sorry."

"She was just a few months older than you."

Tammy could see he wasn't crying, but his face was etched with disbelief, an unmistakable expression of 'how could this happen'-- 'why is life so cruel?' She put her hand on his shoulder. Then she placed her hand under his chin, and raised his head. "Lift your head," she said. "You have nothing to ashamed of. You did all you could, and more."

He pulled her hand down, and shook his head. "I'm going to leave town. I need to find someplace new. When my dad gets out of prison, he's going to want this room back. You're going have to go find your own way, Tammy. I've done all I can." Colton stood and took two steps toward the bedroom door.

"Don't you turn your back on me, Colton King." She grabbed his wrist. "Come back here. Sit down." She pulled him back, and pushed him on the bed. Tammy knelt before him, and put her hands on his knees.

"Let me help you through this. Let me help you carry some of your sadness. I know it won't last. You're too strong a person to let it keep you down." She gazed up at him, and he beheld her bright hazel eyes, and freckles, and sincere expression of caring.

"I've thought the same thing, but I'm so sad."

"Let me help you through it, Colton." She paused for a moment. "I want to be with you. You need me now like I needed you."

"Tammy, it's not like that."

She squeezed his legs together with her arms, and lay her head upon his lap. With puppy dog eyes, wet with tears. "Colton, sweet, Colton. You don't admit to yourself, what I already know. You watch me in the mornings when I brush my teeth and comb my hair, and in the evenings when I get ready for bed. Colton, I'm all woman, and I'm here for you. You needn't be such a perfect gentleman all the time."

"You've been searching for her so long, you've denied yourself. You need someone beside you. You need someone who cares about you. I want to be that person. You saved me. I'm strong and healthy now. And she began to cry, "Colton, I've loved you since the night you took me off the street." She lay her head in his lap. He stroked her hair, then pulled her up to where she sat in his lap, and he held her.

CHAPTER THIRTY-EIGHT

Colton asked Garrison to get him the hospital and police reports, if available, about Marie's last days and hours. A week later, Colton received the information, he knew he didn't want to know. He prayed, she died quickly. He hoped she didn't suffer. He parked his truck in an open lot, sat back in the seat,, and opened the packet.

On March 9, 2012, a young white woman was taken into the ER after she collapsed on the waiting room floor. She had a temperature of 103 degrees, with a heart rate and oxygen intake below normal. Her blood pressure was also extremely weak. Her body showed signs of secondary syphilis infection as she had a rash on her palms and the bottoms of her feet. She had had the infection for a while.

However, the woman died of acute sepsis. The blood infection had progressed beyond the ability of a vigorous antibiotic regimen to stem the damage to vital organs. She passed away on March 18, 2012.

A police investigation identified the name and age of the young woman. She had been working as a prostitute. When she developed a chancre sore on her lip, her handlers knew she was infected. They did nothing, but keep her off the street. When one of them got hold of vials of penicillin, someone gave her several shots, but with dirty needles. She never received any professional medical treatment until the day she collapsed in the ER waiting room.

And on the second page of the report--Colton turned the page--there was a photograph. A 3 X 5 color photo of his Marie. Her thick black hair pulled back from her forehead. The collar of a pink sweater was in view, and on it, a brooch with a pink opal surrounded by a circle of silver petals. Colton held the picture to his chest, leaned his head against the steering wheel, and cried.

CHAPTER THIRTY-NINE

W hen he awoke the next day, Colton sat for a while on the edge of his bed. The life he had planned had been destroyed. Now, he must set a new course for his future. He would do so. His father, Daniel, had been in prison for a year. He would stay with the girls until Daniel was released. Then he would execute his plan. He went into the master bedroom, to the far corner of the large closet, opened the home safe, and retrieved a Glock 9mm handgun. In all of his excursions to Dallas' red light districts, he hadn't ever felt the need for it. Now he would take it with him.

Colton continued to go to his heating and air condition job. Morgan loved her elementary school children, their curious minds, cooperation and attentiveness. Melissa and Christine had become fast friends, and studied together every night. Christine did all she could to clean the house, do laundry, and wash dishes. She was thankful beyond words for the hospitality of the Kings. They had taken her in as one of their own.

Colton and Tammy now slept together in the master bed, and held each other before they fell off to sleep. But there was no sex between them. Tammy had no problem with Colton's lack of interest in sex. She had been penetrated enough times to last a lifetime. It was enough to hold him, to touch him, and experience his kisses. Someday he would want her completely. She could wait. She would wait. Tammy knew he was mindful of her touch, her smell, her tender endearments.

For Colton, Tammy had become his emotional rock. Each day he was drawn to her, more and more, As such, he would not take advantage of her. He would not make sexual relations with her a crass, physical exercise. He would make such a physical commitment between them an act of love-- there, he had just thought it. She was such a sweet person, and he realized he wanted to be around her whenever they weren't working. She was so open emotionally, and he could read her feelings instantly from her bright smile to any hurt or doubt in her mind revealed by her expressive puppy dog eyes. On this Saturday morning, as the girls were fixing breakfast, Colton sat on the bed and thought of all his challenges and responsibilities, and he realized how much he loved Tammy.

CHAPTER FORTY

In July of 2012, word came down that Daniel King had been granted parole. Because of good behavior, he was granted early release though he would have to report to his parole officer for the next three and a half years. He would be assigned to a halfway house for at least ninety days, but his first step back to a normal life was about to happen.

Two days before Daniel's scheduled release date, Colton drove to Spinler, Texas, alone. He had some unfinished business to take care of. He had his cell phone, three feet of ¼" cord, and the 9 mm pistol. It was late afternoon when he arrived in town, and checked into the Happy Trails Motel under a fake ID. He wanted to give the nightly rent to the Vietnamese woman who ran the Cactus Wire Motel, who had helped him so much while he was healing from his burns. But he didn't want her to know he was in town. He lay down to rest, and set the clock alarm to 2:30 am.

In the morning darkness, Colton walked from the

motel. He carried a plastic container, a small crowbar stuck down the outside of his pants, and hung through a belt loop, a small flashlight, the rope, and the loaded pistol. There were several miles to cover to get to 622 Sycamore Lane. He kept to the side streets. When he reached Sycamore, he walked down the middle of the street. At the Rucker's house, he crept along the boundary to escape any motion detectors. He crawled to the house near a corner with no windows, then sat with his back against the brick facade.

Everything was quiet, The field behind the house was quiet. The neighborhood was quiet. The town was asleep. After he caught his breath and stretched, he was ready to get inside. Only one person would be there, Robert Rucker. There were two small windows away from what was obviously the master bedroom with its huge translucent pane in the bath. Colton popped off the screen, and gently pried the plastic frame up the slides. He looked inside the room and found it empty. With a jump, his thighs were over the sill, and he pulled himself into the house.

It was that time in the morning when the sun had yet to break the horizon, but the sky began to glow a hazy, purple-gray. The landscape drew an outline in the distance. Streetlights begin to dim. Colton walked to the cemetery, another mile or two. He could still see a star here and there, and the moon, a hologram on the other side of the sky. He knew where Margie Rucker lay. His pace slowed when he reached the cobblestone path, and he stopped for a while on the narrow wooden bridge to gaze above at the final seconds before dawn. Then, a sliver of rays peeked over the horizon, followed by a mighty curtain of light thrown against the sky, and a new day had begun.

Colton proceeded over the footbridge. Marie would be lying next to her mother. He remembered the bench where he and Marie sat. He knew where his father had been kneeling. And they were there-- headstones side by side.

Marie Ella Rucker
March 13, 1992 ----- March 18, 2012

Colton knelt beside the marker and purged his soul. "I wanted to stop by one more time to tell you were the greatest six weeks of my life. You were a blessing from God. That's why he wanted you back with him so soon. I wish you were with me, but I must move on. You don't need me anymore, because I know you're resting in heaven. Good bye, my angel."

Back at the motel, Colton brushed his teeth and washed up. He would travel to Huntsville and get a motel until tomorrow morning. Melissa had clued him in that she had been writing Daniel letters, all glowing, fabricated reports about how well everything was going back home, To her knowledge, no one had told him about Brenda's death. Colton's heart was weary as he made the drive. He had been thinking about this day for months. He would pick him up and head back to Garland, but there were several things he had to discuss with his father before they arrived back home.

The general belief that a person has paid for their crimes with time served behind bars has always been blatantly misguided. Loss of freedom is society's bill for illegal conduct. It in no way does pays for the carnage, disruption, and heartache felt back home. A penitent attitude does not equal restitution. Only the injured can forgive. The internal strength and abiding love it takes to do so is often drained dry from the human heart.

Colton realized full well, he never would have met Marie if not for his father's infantile pining over a lost love. But equally, his father's presence, his very name, doomed the possibility of them ever having a happy relationship. The in-laws would despise each other, and hate the very ground the other walked on. He had fallen in love with a young woman, so full of life and love, with whom he could never cherish in peace and harmony.

Colton arrived at the prison at noon on the prescribed day, and was directed to a secure parking area. He was searched and held in a waiting room for an hour. He first saw his father as he walked up a sidewalk with a prison guard at his side. Outside the gate, they hugged. Then, they extended their arms, and looked over one another.

"Good to see you, son."

Colton looked back at his father. The man appeared rather tired in the eyes, with long hair to his collar, and a short cropped beard. He'd gotten paunchy in the gut, but still stood with an erect posture. They headed for the car.

'Where is everyone?" Daniel asked.

Back home, eagerly waiting. You've been out of commission for a while. It won't be long now," Colton said. "I have to get you to the halfway house by eight, but there'll be plenty of time for hugs and kisses."

"I tell you, boy. I've learned my lesson. The straight and narrow for me."

"Why don't you call me Colton from now on. I've been taking care of the house for the past year and a half, thanks to your absence, and I'm no longer a boy anyway."

"Okay, sure. If that's what you want."

"I came alone because I have several things I must tell you before we get back." Colton glanced at his father, and Daniel was listening. Any pleasantries or idle words of how he intended to turn over a new leaf was put on hold, and he became fully attentive to what Colton had to say.

"We have a new member of the house. Her name is Christine. I rescued her from the bus station after she ran away from an abusive home. She's the same age as Melissa, and they study together and share the front bedroom. She's going to stay with us for the foreseeable future."

"You've been staying at the house?"

"Of course. I wasn't going to leave all those

women alone without a man around."

"That made it twice as far to your work. Where did you sleep?"

"On the couch. A lot has changed since you've been gone."

Colton saw a sign Rest Area One Mile. "I'm going to pull over." Once they'd pulled in and stopped, Colton took some clothes from the back. "You're not going to the house looking like a convict. Put on these tennis shoes and change your shirt and pants. You need a haircut, too, but that'll have to wait."

As they walked to the truck to leave the rest stop, Colton asked, "When we were in Spinler and you found out your college girlfriend had died, I got to talking to her daughter, Marie, at the cemetery."

"Yes, I couldn't believe how much she looks like her mother. Reminds me of my days with Margie in college."

Colton took a good look at his adoptive father as they got in the truck. Close two years the woman had been dead, and Daniel still talked of her as though she was just out of town.

"Yeah, well . . ." Colton mentally shook his head. "We started seeing each other."

Really! Really?

"Dad, let me ask you . . . Marie mentioned something to me, I've always been curious about. She told me that whenever I met her dad, to say I ate the strawberries. I have met her dad, and we didn't hit it off. He figured out who you were, and he's held it against me. I don't care. But, do you know anything about that--the strawberries? Or maybe she was just playing with me."

Daniel took a moment to think. "No, I don't. That you ate the strawberries . . .? Oh yes, I know. The day you came to their house in the police car, I had snuck in their house. I saw her husband leave and I wanted to see Margie. I was hungry after waiting half the night outside a bedroom window, so I ate what I could find in the refrigerator. I ate a whole bowl of strawberries. Marie caught me in the kitchen. You know the rest."

Colton smiled to himself. For some reason, she had to account for the strawberries so she asked him to accept responsibility. So smart, so resourceful, so sweet. His heart ached at the thought of her. Daniel had the answer to the simple riddle. It was such a minor thing, but Colton cherished Marie's memory even more.

Now, he had to bring up a more serious issue-- the real reason he made the trip alone. They rode for a few miles in silence, then Colton brought up the topic that burned his heart. The man beside him was entirely responsible for his mother's demise, but he forced himself to keep a level tone. He was going to state what happened and why. He would not listen to Daniel's excuses if he started trying to explain away his guilt, and he would not sympathize with him. Once he knew of his wife's passing, Daniel would have to deal with his emotions--alone.

"Mother is gone."

"What do you mean?"

"She died."

"No, no. What happened?"

"She died of a broken heart."

"That's impossible. Melissa's letters said she was working, positive, getting along nicely until I got back."

"Forget Melissa's letters. She wrote them for your benefit at the time, you narrow-minded, self-centered. . . oh my god, mother went into extreme depression from the day you were taken away. She was looking at five years alone, and after all she had done for you. It didn't matter how long you'd be gone, but that you were yanked out of her life at all."

"How did it happen?" Daniel was already plying his face with the fingers on both hands.

"The wrong pills. Too many pills. Does it really matter? We buried her last August." Colton nodded his head. "Yeah, almost a year ago."

"Why didn't you tell me?"

"What for? You think you were going to come to the funeral?"

"This is terrible, terrible, terrible. I was all ready . . ."

"Save it. I don't want to hear it." Colton waited quietly during a ten mile stretch for Daniel to collect his wits. Then he spoke again. "Listen up!" Daniel's head was bowed, his face still in his hands.

"There's one more thing. After Marie and I started seeing each other, her father kidnapped her and sent her away all because I am associated with you. I know she escaped the farm where she was being held, and she made her way to Dallas on the bus. That's how I ran into Christine, at the bus depot, and saved her from exploitation.

"I searched for her night and day, but she died of

a massive blood infection up in Oklahoma City. The autopsy said her body was full of a venereal disease that never received proper treatment. Those worthless sex traffickers used her body, then didn't even get her medical treatment when she was sick." Colton paused. His eyes narrowed, and his voice took on the authority of Moses.

"Pimps are worse than wife beaters. Your only mistake was not killing them. There would have been nobody to identify you."

Daniel looked up from his muddled state. He had caught but a few of Colton's words, but he had heard enough to bring him out of his stupor. "No, Colton, don't think like that. Don't make my mistake. You take out one pimp, and there'll be two to replace him tomorrow. It's an evil of human nature. There's no virtue to it, and there is no end. All you'll ever get is a lengthy sentence or the death chamber. You will never find peace in such a strategy."

"I never said I was going to kill them all."

"Please, please, Colton, don't talk like that. Hasn't my experience shown you the total futility of revenge? Don't make my mistake, son. Don't make my mistake."

Colton kept his focus straight ahead, and didn't reply.

"I want to see my daughters. I want to see my home. I want to go to your mother's grave."

The two men rode in silence the rest of the way home. When they arrived the girls smothered Daniel with hugs and kisses, and introduced Christine and Tammy. Colton sat quietly at the kitchen table and watched the reunion with mixed feelings that would not abate. He would help the man get back on his feet, back as a productive member of society. But more than that, he was reluctant to contemplate. Later that evening, Morgan took Daniel to the halfway house.

CHAPTER FORTY-ONE

Robert Rucker had had a bad dream. He awoke knowing a shadow or a fog had enveloped and touched him. The thought was creepy. The sensation was eerily tactile. He would have sworn, he'd been touched. He had to get ready for work, yet his brain couldn't break his morning stupor, and he went to the kitchen to make a cup of instant coffee.

As soon as he walked into the kitchen, he saw it. Sitting on the counter beside the sink, a plastic container about 3' X 5", maybe two inches deep. Next to the box, a knife stabbed into the Formica counter had cut a strawberry in two. He slowly opened the lid, The box was full of strawberries. It took only an extra second for his whole body to tremble. Someone had been in his house, and he hadn't heard a thing. He could have been murdered in his sleep quickly and silently or subdued and made to suffer a long and painful death. Either notion made him weak, and he slipped in terror to the kitchen floor. He had to get a guard dog, and a pistol in every room. He would call today about a deluxe home security package to monitor every door and window in the house with a siren set on the roof that would go off if anyone entered after he went to bed. His wits were frazzled and his composure crushed when he thought again about what had happened, and yet, he hadn't heard a thing.

Then later, when he had searched the entire house and was late for work, he turned to exit the house. There was a note pinned to the garage door. He read the card, and the truth therein had him once again weak in body, and defeated in spirit, for he realized the truth in the writing, and knew it was all lost forever.

'You will always be a lonely, unimaginative, pitiful soul. The two women in your life, both full of love and understanding, because of you, gave their full measure of affection and devotion to two other men-- men who truly loved them, appreciated them, and felt blessed by their presence.'

CHAPTER FORTY-TWO

Morgan and the younger girls had been planning a fictitious wedding for the past two months. Since Daniel was out of prison, concrete arrangements could move ahead.

Byron had proposed to Morgan at the first of the year. They had been dating for a year prior when they were both seniors at the University of Dallas. Byron was a tall, handsome young man with thinning hair, but big blue eyes, and an engaging smile. He had majored in computer science, and was already working for ViroLogics, Inc. in Dallas.

One evening, Morgan asked Colton to take a walk with her. The evening was still warm, as Texas summer days can be scorching, but there was a breeze, and they began walking with no particular destination in mind.

"So what's up, sis," Colton asked.

Morgan looked up at him, took his arm in hers, and hugged it gently as they walked. She then looked ahead as she spoke. "You know, Colton, a little girl could never have a better big brother than you. I've always been amazed at your dedication to see things through, and tenacity to do what's right. I love you, Colton. I know, you know that, but I wanted to say it."

"Now that dad's home, Byron and I are planning our wedding for September 10th. That's a Sunday afternoon, eight weeks away" She stopped and faced him.

"Colton, I don't want you to just be at my wedding. I want you to make the commitment too-- stand in front of the preacher--say your vows--and marry Tammy."

"What?"

"You heard me," she whispered. "For such an honorable guy, you're as dense as a slab of concrete."

"But."

"Can't you see how much Tammy loves you? She's by your side constantly without demands, because she knows what you've gone through. If you had found Marie, Tammy would have left without a word, she loves you that much."

"What about Byron? What does he have to say?"

"We've already talked about it. Colton, we've both seen you and Tammy together. Don't you even realize how often she makes you smile? You come home from work all tired and sweaty, and the moment you see her, you stand up straight and a big smile comes over you."

Colton stood on the sidewalk, and didn't say a word.

"Oh, Colton, please, please. . . don't let another

sweet, loving woman get away. Don't waste your life pinning over Marie like father did over his college sweetheart."

"I don't intend to."

"Colton, then tell Tammy you love her. I know you do. I know you so well, and I've seen you two together enough to know." Morgan took both of his hands and stood in front of him. "Colton--you've guided me, and nurtured me, and protected me so many times. Let me guide you this time. It would make me so happy to see you marry at the same ceremony as mine."

They turned around and headed back to the house. Morgan said nothing more. She didn't want to repeat herself. Colton understood, but he was a thinker. It would be up to him if Tammy would ever become his wife.

CHAPTER FORTY-THREE

For three days, Colton said nothing about Morgan's admonition. Then one evening, Melissa was showing Tammy how to make a green bean casserole as Colton took a shower. The main course for supper was baked chicken, and when Colton sat down with the girls, he reached around Tammy, and kissed her on the cheek. Never before had Colton been the least bit demonstrative at the dinner table, and all of the girls noticed. Tammy was delighted. Morgan took an even greater note. Colton had combed his hair nicely with a part down the side. He wore an ironed, long-sleeve blue dress shirt. He winked at Morgan after his had served his plate.

When the meal was concluding, Colton looked around the table, and said. "Before everyone gets up, I want you all to know, I picked up a little something this afternoon." He scooted back his chair. "And I think I'll offer it to this pretty little lady, right here." Colton knelt before Tammy, and extended a box in his hand. As Tammy's hands went to her face, Colton opened the box.

"Tammy Dressler, I love you. I want to spend the rest of my life with you. Will you marry me?"

Tammy had the ability to shed tears instantaneously, and this moment was no exception. "Oh, yes, Colton, yes." She fell into his arms almost knocking him off of his feet. The two of them sat on the floor as Colton put the engagement ring on her finger, and Melissa and Christine clapped and cheered while Morgan dabbed mounting tears from the edges of her eyes with a napkin.

Daniel got a job making local deliveries to grocery stores and restaurants for a produce distributor. His days at the halfway house were growing shorter. It wouldn't be long before he'd be back home. He was as excited as the rest of the family in anticipation of a double wedding ceremony. He would have the honor of standing beside Morgan and 'giving her away.' After Byran and Morgan had said their vows and pledged their lives to one another, he would step beside Tammy and 'give her away', as well.

Daniel saw little of the children in the early weeks of his release unless they came downtown to visit him. He seemed to be shaking off the effects of fifteen months incarceration. He visited Brenda's grave several times, always leaving flowers beside her headstone. But the facade of looking to the future came crashing down the afternoon he returned from his produce deliveries smelling like a whiskey distillery. His manager at the company fired him on the spot.

The transgression wasn't enough to send him back to jail, but his parole officer made note of it. Daniel had not been a drinker. When the children were young, Daniel and Brenda never had so much as a bottle of wine in the house. Why had he gotten so soused in the middle of the afternoon that he could have easily wrecked his delivery truck? What brought on this drastic change in his behavior? Colton and Morgan were pretty sure they knew when they got word of the incident. Their father was still living in the past.

CHAPTER FORTY-FOUR

Wedding plans continued in earnest. Colton took money from Daniel and Brenda's savings that, along with contributions from Morgan, Melissa, and Byron, bought Tammy a wedding dress. Melissa would be Tammy's maid of honor, while a friend from school would be Morgans. A couple other friends from school along with Christine completed the number of attendants.

A nearby Methodist church was rented for its ornate chapel. Invitations were sent to Daniel's family members, and the coworkers of each of those who were to take their vows. Even Tammy sent invitations to the three teachers she worked with at the preschool. All of the Kline clan received invitations. Brenda's sisters had taken a special liking to Melissa, being she was Brenda's only birth child, even though she wasn't getting married. They all knew, as well, how much time and effort Brenda had put into raising Colton and Morgan. Those who lived a reasonable distance away RSVP'd they would be in attendance.

The wedding day arrived. Over one hundred people filled the chapel. The organist played Beethoven's Sonata Pathetique as the guest arrived. Daniel escorted Morgan to the traditional sound of the Wedding March followed by a flower girl, one of her elementary school students. Byron had the bearing and posture of a soldier at attention. He smiled lovingly as he took Morgan's hand. Morgan was the embodiment of life and love, and as she and Byron held hands, they faced the preacher, and took their vows.

Then, Daniel went to the back of the chapel, and escorted Tammy to the same solemn march with another of Morgan's young students dropping rose petals behind them. Colton watched her walk down the aisle, his heart welcoming her without any reservations or lingering memories. Tammy had recently turned nineteen. The beauty of youth shown upon her face. The pain she had endured, now washed away by Colton's love and attention. Daniel presented her to the gathered witnesses, and Colton squeezed her hand as they turned and faced the preacher.

Daniel handled his part perfectly, giving away Morgan first, then Tammy with gentle words as though he had raised both of them from newborns. Colton and Tammy were the last to take their vows, and Tammy rushed though her responses so she could get to 'I do,' kiss Colton, then burst into tears.

The reception was held at an Elk's Club a few blocks away from the church. A dance floor took up half of the room with tables and chairs circling it. Along one wall sat an eight-layer wedding cake with a huge punch bowl at the other end of the table. The beverage for the festive occasion was champagne diluted with ginger ale.

Daniel danced with Melissa, and one of the groomsmen danced with Christine. Everyone had a slice of cake, and the shenanigans that accompany a wedding reception began to a chorus of titters, then outright laughter.

Daniel began hanging around the punch bowl. A beaker from his jacket pocket added vodka to his drink, and by time the flask was empty, Daniel was adding nothing from the punch bowl to his glass but ice. When the DJ called for quiet, both married couples took to the dance floor, and in the solemn occasion, danced together as bride and groom.

Judy Kline Hall, Brenda's youngest sister got another slice of cake. As she passed the punch bowl, Daniel's tipsiness was in evidence, and Judy snorted a remark.

"Can't you act like a responsible adult for three hours?" When he glanced her way, Judy shot back an icy stare. "Good grief, King. Your children are getting married, and you can't even stand up straight?"

Daniel glared back at her. "Why don't you shut up, and go feed your face?" Daniel intended to step toward her, but when he stood, he twisted his foot, and he fell into the table. The twenty-quart glass serving bowl crashed to the floor. The bowl disintegrated in a shower of glass pellets, and with several gallons of punch behind it, washed halfway across the floor.

The married couples quit dancing. The music stopped. Total silence descended upon the gathering. Everyone looked at Daniel who quickly turned away. He staggered to a nearby wall, and with his arm extended against it for balance, lowered his head. Even then, he appeared unsteady. Colton hurried over and stood beside him.

"What happened?"

"You'll never forget, Marie," Daniel said. You can try all . . ."

"What?" At first the words sounded like gibberish. Colton felt certain he had misunderstood his father's words. But then, in the next instant, the words hit his brain like a lightening bolt. Total dismay immediately turned into righteous anger, and he wanted to hit the man. "What the hell is wrong with you?" He stepped back, and pointed. "Get him out of here."

Colton was so astonished, so flabbergasted, he shook. Why would Daniel say such a thing? The man was in torturous, everlasting emotional pain, but what kind of callused heart throws that kind of remark at someone on their wedding day? He had taken Tammy to love and cherish, not because he had to, but because life goes on. A few of Colton's friends and coworkers ushered Daniel from the building.

Initially, Colton thought he'd been stabbed, so painful were his father's words. But, he would not let his father's wallowing in the past ruin his wedding day. He walked back over to Tammy, kissed her, and motioned the DJ to restart the song.

Even as a few guests cleaned up the mess, Colton held Tammy tightly. "I love you, Mrs. King. I love you."

CHAPTER FORTY-FIVE

Daniel's remark quickly spread among the attendees at the wedding reception. A lot of head shaking resulted along with some choice words, even threats against Daniel. But while the reception got a black eye, the ceremonies were a huge success. Byron and Morgan headed to Vail, Colorado, for their honeymoon. Colton took Tammy to Galveston, for theirs.

One evening while in Galveston, Colton and Tammy sat on the balcony of their suite overlooking the Gulf of Mexico.

"Sweetheart," Tammy said, "May I ask you something?"

Colton just looked back, her voice gained his full attention.

"Can we move from Dallas? I have a bad vibe about the city. I'd like to start someplace new."

Colton took her hand. "Where did you have in mind?"

"I love Louisiana. I don't want to go to Shreveport where my parents are, but anywhere else. You'll love it, too, Colton. I promise. Maybe some-place like Monroe."

Colton reached over and pulled her into his arms. "You're so sweet," he said. "Do you think I care where we live as long as I have you?"

Tammy reached around his chest and lay her head on his shoulder. She said nothing more, but as they both gazed out toward the water, she placed a tender kiss upon his cheek.

When Colton and Tammy returned from their honeymoon, Colton told the younger girls of their intention to move away. Immediately, apprehension sprang from Melissa's face, and Colton realized he had a problem he hadn't considered.

"No," Melissa said. "You can't move away."

"Why not, precious. You know, we just got married."

"I don't want you to."

"Tammy wants to move to Louisiana."

"Well then you'll . . .Colton, you can't leave me with dad. He's not making any money–to support two girls. He'll send Christine home. He'll have to. Colton, I can't deal with him alone."

"What about your friends at school?"

"Colton, I'm serious. Don't move. But if you go, take me with you. And Christine."

Colton pulled Melissa to him and hugged her. "Don't worry. I'll never abandon you. Dad might get-a-grip and take advantage of the time early parole has given him. Or he may go languish in his toxic memories. But you're right, it's not a job for you alone. Morgan will still be around, but maybe, just maybe, being alone in an empty house might be dad's best therapy."

Colton looked at Tammy, and she was smiling. "Okay then, girls. Pack your bags. We're headed to Louisiana."

When Morgan learned of their plans, she too objected.

"Daniel, what am I supposed to do without you around? Dad's more melancholy now than I've ever seen him."

"Well, what can I do?" Daniel replied. "After that stunt he pulled at the reception, I need a break from him. I just got married, you know. Tammy wants to go to Louisiana."

"I just got married too," her tone grew in force and urgency. "Maybe we should have told him about mom's overdose when it happened. He would have had time to adjust to the loss." Morgan's eyes implored Colton to stick around Dallas. "We owe him."

"Oh, you're going to throw that at me?" He looked up at the sky and exhaled deeply. "He's not elderly, you know. What is he, forty-one? He can find another woman. Just because he's wallowing in his troubles at the moment, doesn't mean he can't snap out of it, and make a new start."

"And how is that going to happen?"

Colton didn't hesitate. "I say, pull the rug out from under him. Give him a dose of tough love. Make him stand on his own two feet and he'll snap out of it sooner than babysitting his sorrows and regrets."

Morgan's expression didn't change.

"I mean, everyone makes mistakes," Colton said, "fail at things, wish they had done things differently."

"So you're going to leave me alone with him to deal with?"

"You don't have to deal with him at all if you don't want to. He still has friends. Garrison still likes him." Colton paused for a moment. "I'm sorry, but Tammy and I are moving, and Melissa and Christine want to come with us."

Morgan gave him the most disappointed stare he had ever witnessed from his little sister. "I thought more of you, Colton," she said. "I never really thought you'd bail on someone in need."

CHAPTER FORTY-SIX

Three days later the girls loaded up the bed of Colton's truck with all they could take. Daniel and Morgan were there for goodbyes. Melissa and Christine were excited about a change in scenery. Colton and Tammy were excited about starting a new life.

Colton knew he was leaving behind two middle-aged men, both alone, both harnessed with memories that would never fade or change. He knew Marie's father, Robert Rucker, now living alone in Spinler wasn't worth killing. Let him suffer with the thoughts of what he'd lost, what he'd neglected, and taken for granted. Colton doubted that any other woman would have anything to do with him, if they knew of his morose and self-centered nature.

With Daniel it was different. Colton loved the man dearly, but he would not be a party to his juvenile, destructive, and constant dwelling in the past. The man had changed his life for the better, and the man had made his life a living hell. Colton prayed he would look to the future, and chart a new life. He was still a young man. Morgan would be nearby to help, but Daniel's personal fulfillment, would be up to him, and him alone.

Melissa held Daniel tightly, and kissed him. "I love you, daddy."

Morgan watched stone faced as she watched them pack. She hugged all the girls, but said very little. Daniel's mind seemed preoccupied. He expressed no well wishes for their new destination or for a safe trip. When all was ready to go, Colton went to Daniel.

"Take care of yourself, dad. You have a new lease on life with a thousand opportunities before you." Colton stood before him for a moment, then hugged the older man. "We'll keep in touch. I promise."

"Don't worry about me, Daniel said. "I think I'll go away myself."

"You're going to sell the house?" Colton asked, somewhat surprised.

"We'll see."

Colton, Tammy, Melissa, and Christine stopped in Ruston, Louisiana, and decided to begin their new lives there. They rented a three-bedroom house and got the younger girls enrolled in high school. Colton easily got on with a heating and air conditioning company. Tammy wanted to go back to school, but she had none of the necessary paperwork for enrollment. For the time being, she stayed at the house, cooked, and took care of the others, especially Colton.

A month later, Colton got a call from Bryon. As soon as he heard the tone of Byron's voice, Colton knew it was bad news.

"I'm so sorry to have to tell you, Colton. . ." Even Byron's voice cracked at the words he had to say. ". . . your father hung himself this morning from the eave overhanging the back porch."

Immediately, Colton felt weak. The phone burned against his ear, and the room seemed to spin.

"Morgan?"

"She's asleep now. The doctor gave her a sedative. It was a neighbor who found him. I'm at the house now, and the police are still here."

Silence overtook the line while Colton collected his thoughts. "All right," he finally said. "I'll head in tomorrow morning. See if he can be buried next to Brenda. Let Morgan know I'm coming. Let's get this over as quickly as possible."

"Sorry, I had to deliver such bad news," Bryon said.

"It's all right. Thanks for relieving Morgan of the chore. It was always at the back of my mind, Byron, but god knows I prayed countless times that it wouldn't turn out this way. I'll see you in the morning."

Three days later, Colton sat with Morgan and Byron on the front row as the preacher delivered a sermon on the life of a good man. The funeral director had provided him with the specifics about the deceased's time on earth. The casket remained closed.

The words droned across the chapel as Colton thought about the man he both loved and despised. He would have done anything to save his adopted father from himself, but the spirit of personal redemption had not found root in his father's heart.

The man had lost his career and his wife in large part due to bad decisions of his own making. But Colton knew, the lingering sadness and unmitigated despair that destroyed his will to live came from the loss of his first love, a girl he knew in college and never got over, even after her death more than two years ago. While in prison, his mind was probably taken up with other things. But once he was released, and all of his family had moved on to lives of their own, the memory of the girl from college returned to haunt him. The emotional struggle was useless. There was no reason to go on for he would never have his precious Margie.

Colton said his goodbyes to Morgan and Bryon that evening, but spent one more night in the house he knew as his boyhood home. He walked through the house recalling memories. Morgan would handle getting the place sold. He had trouble getting to sleep. He tossed and turned all night, and finally got up for good at 5 am.

Colton headed east, back toward Louisiana. Once again, he witnessed the majestic spectacle of sunrise. Like spikes on a crown, rays of sun pierced the horizon. Shadows of darkness evaporated before the early light, and the sky began to brighten. Soon, Colton was driving into the risen sun. The light was a beacon unto him. The dawn signaled a future of wonderful possibilities. Tammy was waiting for his return, and Colton felt the sweet savor of life and the promise of the morning.